EXPOSED!

Don't miss the first book in the exciting
BEVERLY HILLS, 90210 series

Beverly Hills, 90210

And, coming soon

Beverly Hills, 90210—No Secrets

**Published by
HarperPaperbacks**

BEVERLY

90210

HILLS

™

SPELLING ENT. INC.

EXPOSED!

BART AND NANCY MILLS

HarperPaperbacks
A Division of HarperCollins*Publishers*

HarperPaperbacks   *A Division of* HarperCollins*Publishers*
10 East 53rd Street, New York, N.Y. 10022

Cover photo by Andrew Semel
Back cover photos by Timothy White
Insert photos by Andrew Semel and Timothy White.
First printing: December 1991

Printed in the United States of America

HarperPaperbacks and colophon are trademarks of HarperCollins*Publishers*

10 9 8 7 6 5 4 3 2 1

Contents

**BASED ON THE TELEVISION SERIES CREATED
BY DARREN STAR**

A word-of-mouth hit

DYLAN: Welcome to the real world, Brandon.
BRANDON: Why does Beverly Hills have this effect on people?
DYLAN: Hey, don't put this off on Beverly Hills. These problems go way back!

Not many people found "Beverly Hills, 90210" the night it first aired. The show's title didn't indicate that it was about high school. It wasn't on one of the three major networks. It didn't have any high-profile stars. There wasn't much promotion behind it. The critics hardly mentioned it.

But the show's audience grew week by week as more and more young viewers discovered it. Soon it became the main Friday-morning topic of conversation in high schools across the country. Word of mouth spread, and before long the junior high kids were tuned in. Even college kids began deserting "Cheers" to watch the show that told the truth about that inferno of emotions they had recently escaped—high school. Eventually, by the summer of 1991, "Beverly Hills, 90210" had the majority of American teenagers tuned in on Thursdays at 9:00 P.M. And word has it that some parents are even taking a look—a few have complained that the show is too real for their poor protected darlings. Clearly "Beverly Hills, 90210" is a phenomenon—the new hot show of the nineties.

Why? It could be the dishy guys, the lustrous Jason Priestley, the mysterious Luke Perry. Or the lovely, headstrong Shannen Doherty, so easy for young women to identify with. More likely, though, the show attracts a passionately devoted youthful audience because it tells the truth. Not the whole truth—this is television. Not nothing but the truth, because a little fantasy makes the whole package more attractive. But enough of the truth so that American teenagers can for the first time say that TV is taking them seriously.

"Beverly Hills, 90210" doesn't treat teens' problems as inconveniences for the adults in their lives or as chances for the adults to show off their sensitivity. When young people have problems, their lives are consumed by them, and the one thing they don't want to hear is "That's nothing. Wait till you grow up if you want problems."

Romance may be a problem for adults, but no romantic problem in anyone's life is as serious as first love. Adults face moral dilemmas all the time, but few choices later in life are as hard to make as whether to cheat in class. "Beverly Hills, 90210" dramatizes these and countless other adolescent problems with sensitivity and seriousness.

The show also avoids preaching and offering easy answers. The after-school special genre is notorious for edging up toward the real problems of teenagers and solving them with the stroke of a pen. "Beverly Hills, 90210" demonstrates that there are as many ways to handle problems as there are kids. The show concedes that there are some problems that kids just can't solve.

In the real world of "Beverly Hills, 90210," authority figures make mistakes. A teacher is incompetent. A mother is an addict. Even the supertraditional parents at the center of the show, the Walshes, are often wrong. Sometimes they deserve to be lied to. They're learning as much as their kids, episode by episode.

How did it happen? Who are these people?

GIRL AT THE BEACH: You're really nice!
BRANDON: Yeah, well, I'm from out of town.

It started very quietly last season. Without much fanfare, the up-and-coming "fourth network," Fox Broadcasting, launched its new hour-long program aimed at the "fourteen-to-eighteen demographic"—teenagers, for short.

It was to be the first television program to dramatize the problems and joys of the high school years from the kids' perspective. It would thus be a real shift in perspective for prime-time television. Virtually every high school classroom ever seen in TV series in the past was shot from the front of the room—that is, from the teacher's perspective. Think of "Welcome Back, Kotter" and "Head of the Class." The kids could be stars, too, but their story lines were secondary to the teachers'. The kids actions were judged by adults, and the adults held all the power.

But that was fantasy land, and Fox Broadcasting had figured it out. Kids' problems today are most often solved by the kids, if they are solved at all. What matters most to kids is the opinion of their peers. For the majority of kids, adults exist as encumbrances or obstacles, not as wise advisers or role models.

If Fox could shoot a series that placed the camera in the back of the classroom—that is, if the show observed high school from the kids' perspective—then the network might have a winner. To paraphrase *Field of Dreams*, Fox figured, if you shoot it, they will watch.

Cleverly, the network decided to set the show in a real place that would look like a fantasy: Beverly Hills, California. With its stratospheric median income, its mind-boggling shopping opportunities, its row on row of mansions worth tens of millions of dollars, Beverly Hills is ostentatious wealth taken to a ridiculous extreme. At the same time, the citizens of Beverly Hills put on their expensive stone-washed jeans one leg at a time. People are people, after all.

So the show's gimmick would be to depict extremely real problems in a virtually fake place. If a car gets stolen, it should be a top-of-the-line Corvette. If a boy gets drunk, it should be on mango margaritas. If kids go to the beach, they should lounge in an exclusive beach club with uniformed cabana boys.

The gimmick has worked before, on television with "The Beverly Hillbillies" and in the movies with *Beverly Hills Cop*. The variation in this show was to bring a "normal" family into this hotbed of conspicuous consumption. We'd see how homespun midwestern virtue rubbed against all that phony Far West glitz.

The Out-of-Towners

BRENDA: How many days in a row can you go shopping before you're declared brain dead?

The Walshes of Minneapolis arrived in Beverly Hills without a vice to their name. They were plain, thrifty, low-key, friendly, generous ordinary people. They certainly didn't belong here!

But their children were more adaptable, more open to the allure of this Shangri-la. Brandon and Brenda wanted to have friends and fit into their new school. Who wouldn't? Brenda needed the wardrobe to make her acceptable to the cool girls at school, and shoplifting looked like a quick and easy short-cut. Brandon had always been the stronger of the twins, but the temptations of Beverly Hills seduced him, too, more than once. In fact, "The Seduction of Brandon" could be a subtitle of the series, for if the temptation wasn't fast cars or too much booze, it was wild women or even older wild women. Brandon's conscience clicked in and out and became one main-spring of the show.

Meanwhile Brenda wavered between the superfi-ciality of the campus-queen set she worked hard to join and the bedrock of her built-in core morality. It wasn't long, though, before she stopped worrying so much about externals and started counting her heartbeats. Her romance with Dylan was slow to build, soon to explode, ever afterward to bubble on and off. Although "Beverly Hills, 90210" has many other elements that progress from episode to episode, the primary cliff-hanger is the progress of Brenda's romance with Dylan McKay.

Dylan, surprisingly, became the show's wild card. Missing from the pilot, originally written in for just a single episode, the character immediately struck audiences as the paragon of fascinating dan-ger. Every school has a Dylan—a misfit miscreant with a murky past and a possibly tragic future. Nothing can save a man like Dylan, except perhaps the love of a good woman.

The show's creators surrounded the leads with strong sidekicks and antagonists. To lead Brandon into temptation, there is the golden boy with the empty soul, Steve Sanders. As the girl who goads Brandon into listening to his better angels, there is his secret admirer, activist interloper Andrea Zuckerman. To personify the specious attractions of Beverly Hills, there is Kelly Taylor, superbitch-in-training. As Kelly's sidekick, the ditzy Donna Martin. As Steve and Kelly's wannabe buddy, the pushy David Silver.

All of these characters echo every viewer's high school experience. Brandons abound—boys who seem too good to be true and become all the more attractive when they have a little egg on their faces. There's a Brenda on the left of you and a Brenda on the right—girls who know love when they see it but aren't sure how to express it. Everybody knows a Steve and hates him—and envies his cocksureness. A Kelly runs the top girls' clique in every school, impenetrably beautiful but sometimes allowing a hint of humanity to show through. An Andrea bustles along every corridor, finding fault, being irritatingly right—and once in a while letting down her guard. Girls like Donna hover emptily in the orbit of the most beautiful people—but you know what? They can be funny. You're aware of the David Silvers of the school like a pebble in your shoe, but you'll probably find yourself voting for David for class president one of these days.

The actors who portray these almost mythic types are as mixed a group as the characters themselves. They were brought together by the show's producers in a harrowing and cutthroat casting process. They were plunked into story lines that assumed relationships they had to simulate instantly. As Luke Perry said of Dylan's romance with Brenda, "Shannen and I were thrust into this together . . . ."Wham! 'You guys are in love.'"

Jason Priestley was the producers' biggest gamble. Jason was their first choice, but because he was under contract to another series at the time they signed him only for the pilot of "Beverly Hills, 90210." If the other show, "Sister Kate," had been renewed, "Beverly Hills, 90210" would have had to recast its male lead.

Jason's portrayal of Brandon is a real acting job, for he's very far from being a naive moralist. Jason is actually a tearaway thrill-seeker, and proud of it, man. He goes at competitive hockey and bungee jumping (falling off high bridges while attached to a length of elastic) with reckless abandon. On the "Beverly Hills, 90210" set, Jason is always the life of the party, urging the cast and crew on to ever greater, ever speedier accomplishments. He's an extrovert and a leader.

Shannen Doherty had the strongest acting background of any of the cast. Others spent their childhood picking up pin money acting; Shannen has been a veritable star for most of her teen years. Only twenty, she was best known before "Beverly Hills, 90210" for her role in "Our House" on TV. In films, she played the dominating Heather in that black-on-black comedy, *Heathers*.

She, too, differs significantly from her character. Brenda has had a sheltered upbringing, but Shannen has been interacting professionally with adults for half her life. Brenda is a largely reactive character, responding to challenges from outside, but Shannen is out there, ready to stir things up on her own. Brenda agonizes over what she should do; Shannen is far more certain of herself. Brenda and Dylan are lovers; Shannen and Luke Perry took a long time to find each other's rhythm.

As for Luke, he's the rankest outsider in the group. He auditioned in a borrowed shirt without buttons because he was called in suddenly from his construction job. He had come from Ohio, trailing a rebellious past. He'd grown up relating more closely to television icons like Starsky and Hutch than to real adults in his hometown.

Externally, Luke and Dylan don't have much in common. Luke would never borrow Dylan's wardrobe, being more comfortable in jeans and T-shirt. Inside, however, Luke carries a lot of Dylan's angst and anger. Dylan is a compulsive truth-teller, and so is Luke. Dylan hides his intellect behind a self-destructive facade. Luke hides his behind a soft-spoken everyday vocabulary. But there are differences, too. Dylan might go off the rails; Luke has passed that point in his life. Dylan seems to stay moody even when he's having fun; Luke loves to let his hair down and often shows his enjoyment. Dylan keeps to himself; Luke is a great mixer.

Ian Ziering took the longest route to join the "Beverly Hills, 90210" cast, having grown up and lived in the New Jersey suburbs of New York City. He was a child actor, a success onstage, in commercials and on daytime dramas. He even once lost out to Luke Perry when they were both up for the same part in a soap audition in New York.

Steve Sanders is the life of any party at West Beverly High, and Ian Ziering is the light show any day of the week on the "Beverly Hills, 90210" set. His energy and love of life are infectious, and he is by unanimous vote of the rest of the cast "the funniest man alive." The difference between Ian and his character is that Steve has been neglected by his parents and hence has no moral center, no rudder to steer by, so most of his attractive energy goes into hurtful thoughts or deeds whereas, Ian talks lovingly of his long-married parents and stresses the good lessons they taught him.

Jennie Garth is another performer who has worked hard to create a character very unlike herself. She grew up around horses—first on a horse farm in Illinois, later in Phoenix. Going into show business was a freak accident in her life. "Beverly Hills, 90210" is her first big break.

Unlike Kelly Taylor, Jennie remains unaffected, spontaneous, down-to-earth. Kelly would kill to possess the right dress; Jennie's values are more home-rooted. Kelly's mother is a recovering alcoholic who is just discovering her own daughter; Jennie's mother shepherded her through her introduction to show business, and Jennie's father's influence remains strong, too. Kelly inspires envy; Jennie simply offers friendship.

Gabrielle Carteris plays an outsider in Beverly Hills, and that's what she is, too. She grew up in northern California, where she was "a hippie cheer-leader," and she came of age in and around New York and London. She endured many disparaging remarks from agents and casting directors before proving that she could be a professional.

Andrea Zuckerman can be irritatingly self-righteous—at least, she sometimes strikes Brandon that way. Gabrielle has some strong opinions, too, but she doesn't push them in people's faces as Andrea does. Emotionally, Andrea is a little backward, uncertain how to express her feelings toward Brandon; Gabrielle is usually quite sure of herself. The actress and the character are alike in their compulsion to cram everything they can into their lives.

For Brian Green, playing pushy freshman David Silver came naturally: he just remembered the way he was himself four years before and put some of it on the screen. Brian has been an actor since he was six, in commercials and TV dramas, most notably "Knots Landing."

David Silver is a character with a lot of room to grow, a kid who won't ever quit trying to peek in the older kids' windows. He's extra-high-energy, and he puts nonstop effort into doing all the wrong things. Likewise, Brian is a can't-sit-still guy, but he's very self-aware, too. All the others in the cast envision Brian emerging into greater prominence in the future.

Tori Spelling is the only cast member who has actually lived a life like her character's. She comes from Beverly Hills and went to a local private school, Westlake School for Girls. She has been acting since she was six, mostly in episodes of TV series like "Vega$" and "The Wizard." She's been in a feature film, *Troop Beverly Hills,* and she has written, directed and starred in her own short film.

Tori, too, likes to shop. However, shopping for Donna is a moral imperative, while for Tori it's a pleasure and a diversion. The function of Donna originally was simply to reflect Kelly's glory, but Tori has been able to build the part into something more with her left-field sense of humor.

This is the way the day starts

IT'S A LATE MORNING FOR THE "BEVERLY Hills, 90210" cast and crew. It's past nine-thirty and the fun hasn't even begun! Usually everyone arrives at the clubhouse—I mean, the studio—on the early side of the rush hour. But today hangout time—that is, the cast's makeup call—starts at midmorning. So nobody's here first thing in the morning except the phone answerers and the not-so-secret admirers of Jason and Luke.

"Here" is a nondescript supersecret building located somewhere deep in the San Fernando Valley, where "Beverly Hills, 90210" shoots most of its indoor scenes. It's not too close to a freeway and not too far from Hollywood, on the other side of the Santa Monica Mountains from the real Beverly Hills.

From the outside, the building looks like just another warehouse, but it's actually a fully equipped television soundstage.

Brandon's and Brenda's bedrooms, with the famous connecting bathroom, form the centerpiece of the roomy interior of the structure. Various other parts of the Walsh household stand at odd angles, unlit and looking abandoned.

At the front of the building, members of the office staff await everybody's arrival. Much gum-chewing and nail-filing occurs. The cast and crew call is late today because the show was shooting on location very late the night before. The crew's union rules require a lengthy break between one day's shoot and the next, so it's already nine-thirty . . . but wait! Heeeeeeeere's Jason!

Jason's outfit is a bit wilder than anything Brandon would permit himself to wear. His wild tie-dyed shirt hangs loose from his shoulders. None of the young women answering the phones fails to say hello. He picks up his personal mail—his fan mail comes separately in a truck.

Among the letters and notes there's a small book-sized package. Curious, he opens it. It's a tome about the Mormon Church, and Jason shows it around for everyone's amusement. "Someone put me on the list, and I get all this literature," he explains. "I'm reading up, you bet! Soon I'll start my own religion!"

Jason goes off to Makeup to get down-aged to high school years. Shannen Doherty strides through the door, a little bit late and all business. She's wearing skin-hugging black bicycle shorts and a black duckbill cap (on a boy it would be a baseball hat). Shannen heads straight for Makeup.

Gabrielle Carteris breezes in, bringing the kind of personality that lifts the edges of piles of paper. She's lugging a big bag with some of her ever-present reading matter and a change of clothes. She's just come from the circus. "I'm so sore!" she says, smiling at the pain of it all.

Gabrielle hasn't been watching the circus; she's been *in* the circus. She doesn't have enough to do at work seventy or eighty hours a week, so she spends a bunch of time learning to walk the high wire. How thick is that wire? someone asks her. She makes a fist with a little hole, indicating a very thin wire, almost unwalkable-on. "Bye, guys!" she yells, hustling to the microwave in the studio kitchenette. "I'm going to get a vegetable burrito—want something?"

Later, work is occurring. Men are climbing up and down ladders. They're carrying loads back and forth. They're putting things on top of other things. This is known as filmmaking! At any given time half of a film crew will be moving around looking very busy indeed and the other half will be playing hackysack in the back.

The first shot today is in Brandon's bedroom, so that's where the hurry-scurry is centered. Have you ever seen the ceiling of Brandon's bedroom, or wished you had? Well, you haven't, because there isn't any ceiling. There is space to set lights. There is the business end of an oversize yellow python that turns out to be an air-conditioning tube connected to a cold-air generator thirty feet away.

You have seen the walls of his room, and you're used to the Minnesota Vikings poster and the Neville Brothers poster. Have you noticed the "Elect Brandon Walsh Junior Class President" poster on the inside of his closet door?

The episode director, Jeff Melman, and two or three others are lying in the "window" of the bedroom while the crew fine-tunes the lighting for this scene, aiming the spots at stand-ins who are the same height and coloring as "the first team."

"Bring 'em in," goes the call, and the first team—Jason, Shannen, and Jennie Garth—appears on the set. They've come in from their dressing rooms, past the sign pointing back to "Neuro Psychiatric Ward." The girls are wearing cute cutoffs and hiking boots. Jason is in jeans and a sweater. Everybody calls him Jay or Jace.

"It's your worl', squirrel!" barks the director to Jason. "Ain't no thing but a chicken wing!"

"Let's do it!" agrees Jason. He's flexing a handexerciser in preparation for his role in *Terminator 3*. (Just kidding!)

It's a scene from the episode where Brandon and Brenda lead the gang on a camping and hiking trip. Right now they're packing. Brandon is rummaging in his closet for his lucky hat. He's standing on a sawhorse that the camera doesn't quite see. The makeup person, wearing a chain of daisies in her hair—apparently in honor of the episode's camping motif—hurries around the set primping the principals.

Jason and Jennie horse around, arm in arm, waiting out the last minutes before the time-to-shoot shouts go up: "Rolling! Speed! Marker! Action!"

They do the scene. Then they do the scene again. Then, for a change, they do the scene again. After that, they do it again.

Jason announces, "We're in coverage, ladies and gentlemen!" He means he'd like to be in coverage ("coverage" means close-ups, which are always shot after the scene is filmed from a wider angle). Jason is always a little bit quicker than everyone else, a little bit readier to move things along.

"One more time," the teacher—I mean, the director—says. The actors do it again, and afterward Jason needles, "That's a wrap. Let's all go home!"

"I'm happy with that scene," the director concedes.

"I'm just sooooo happy with that scene," Jennie mocks, poking Shannen playfully and getting herself chased all around the set.

Later—much later—all eight principals are squeezed onto a tiny set representing the cabin to which Brandon and Brenda have dragged the group. They've just come out of the "rain" to see this dilapidated lean-to where they'll have to stay. An elaborate system of tubes is attached to the ceiling to simulate a leak in the roof.

The long-suffering director is trying to corral eight free spirits into one tight group and move them around like chess pieces. Jennie is doing the pogo and trilling nonsense syllables to loosen up. "Thespians in position!" the director calls. "This is going to be hard enough. We don't need everybody talking."

Down to business. They run their lines. They rehearse their moves. Jason comes up with a slight change in his lines that sharpens their meaning, and the director heartily approves. Ian donates one of his best lines to Luke. The whole group is full of useful suggestions for making the complicated choreography work. This is a humming team!

Quicker than a teacher's frown, the scene is blocked and ready for the camera. While the electricians go about their final work, Ian, Jason, and Brian are found sitting on the bed. No warning, no cues. Ian says, "Here we go, guys," and jumps up and lands hard on his butt on the bed. Jason, next in line, goes up and lands hard on his butt on the bed. Jason comes down and Brian shoots up and lands hard with his butt on the bed. Something inside the bed cracks. The guys crack up.

The pause before shooting goes on. The cry goes up, "Cast! Get damp!" This time, instead of being made up, the actors have to get wet down. After all, they're coming in out of the rain. The make-up people have spritzer guns loaded with Evian water. Shannen grabs one of the bottles and sprays like Machine Gun Kelly. David is in her line of fire and promises, "You're gonna get it . . . sometime. You won't know when!"

The bell rings. The red light goes on.

"Action!" "Cut!" "Action!" "Cut!"

And so it goes.

Heavy thoughts and history— but this won't be on the test

NEW YORK TIMES: "Beverly Hills, 90210" is "Thirtysomething" for teenagers. . . . It effectively touches the problems of teenagers. . . . The characters confront their problems with honesty.

VARIETY: Regular viewers of the show have come to depend on it for humor, true-to-life depictions of teens (well, at least rich ones) and an open mind.

ROLLING STONE: The show owes its success to its unconventional approach to teenagers: it takes them seriously.

The television schedule is full of programs aimed at teenagers, but all except one are half-hour situation comedies. The listings are stuffed with shows set in school, but all except one are half-hour situation comedies. Do you ever get the idea that television doesn't take teenagers seriously?

Television's idea of young adults is that they are inconveniences except when they're funny. In some shows they're on the screen just to show that the adult characters aren't gay. In most others they're on the screen to give the adult characters an excuse to show how caring and wise they are. Hey, I'm not knocking Kirk Cameron, but where are the teen characters on TV who have more depth than a dishrag?

"Beverly Hills, 90210" was conceived to compete dramatically with "thirtysomething" and "L.A. Law"—shows that mix comedy and drama into an entertaining version of reality. "Beverly Hills, 90210" is the first hour-long teen comedy-drama. It's a format in which highly charged drama and flat-out comedy coexist, just as they do in real life.

"When Fox came to me," recalls series creator Darren Star, "they wanted a high school show that had never been done before. It had to be honest and thoughtful and treat its characters with respect. There have been shows in that vein on TV about cops, about doctors, about lawyers—about everybody but teenagers."

It doesn't take a 4.0 GPA to figure out that high school is just four years, for most people, and high school kids form a fairly small proportion of the whole TV audience. That means, watch out, ratings might suffer. Well, excuuuuuse me!

But Fox is a venturesome new network willing to

try to carve out new niches for itself. Nobody thought "The Simpsons" would be a hit and so forth and so forth. The network's original concept for "Beverly Hills, 90210" grew out of its ownership of the merchandising rights to Beverly Hills High School. That's right, in Los Angeles a high school can have merchandising rights. You may be wearing a BHHS T-shirt right now. BHHS could be the only high school with a working oil well on its campus, pumping revenue directly into the classrooms.

Alas, the network discovered that its BHHS rights didn't actually cover portraying the school on TV. That's how the famous fictional West Beverly High School came to be invented. There's really only one high school in Beverly Hills—BHHS. But there are lots of private schools, as you might expect, that cater to the city's many richies.

"'Beverly Hills' was the show's original hook," recalls Darren Star. "The pitfall I wanted to avoid was making a show that was as glitzy and empty as people's stereotype of Beverly Hills. I wanted to show that stereotype—and then play against it. A lot of clichés are true. There is a lot of empty glitz in Beverly Hills. But there is real life, too, and that's what I wanted to show."

Star is from the Maryland suburbs of Washington, D.C. He and his sister, one year younger, went to Walt Whitman High School, in the wealthiest part of wealthy Montgomery County. "I knew what it was like to be Brandon and Brenda, coming from a solid, value-oriented family into a fast-lane school. 'Beverly Hills' is a state of mind that exists everywhere.

That's why kids everywhere identify with the characters in this show. What happens at West Beverly happens everywhere."

Star wrote, and Aaron Spelling produced a pilot, geared for early in the evening. The director was Tim Hunter, who had made *Tex,* with Matt Dillon, and *River's Edge,* with Keanu Reeves. But TV's unwritten rules forbid too much reality too early in the evening—you never know who might be watching!—so the serious side of the characters was soft-pedaled.

When the pilot got picked up and the show went to series, the scenario and characters were toughened up. Rebel Dylan McKay was thrown into the mix. That was when the show really became "teensomething." That was when it established its pattern of forthrightly showing the perils of growing up today without preaching or offering phony easy answers.

An alumnus of Beverly Hills High School, Chuck Rosin, came on board as executive producer. "I'm thirty-nine," he admits, "but I remember. I remember. There was Junior-Senior Night. We used that as the background for the show where Brenda counsels the date-rape victim. BHHS really has a mother-daugher fashion show, and we used that. We used BHH'S Hello Day, a welcoming day with skits.

"I know the subject matter well, although the Beverly Hills I grew up in no longer exists, unfortunately. Twenty years ago the school was the focus of the community. Sometime in the mid-seventies, Rodeo Drive became the focus. People used to move to Beverly Hills because of the schools. Rich people began moving in to be near the other rich people. Property values rose sky-high, and many of the new families didn't have kids. Enrollment went down.

"We used to have the top school in California. BHHS isn't the best any more. It still has the planetarium, but there's nobody to teach astronomy. So the show has a nostalgic quality for me. West Beverly is in some ways more like the private schools on the West Side than the real BHHS."

But the students on "Beverly Hills, 90210" and their hopes and fears are very true to life. Plenty of kids, like Steve Sanders, have a neglectful show biz parent. Other kids, like Dylan McKay, have absentee parents obsessed with their own business. Some parents, like Kelly Taylor's, have substance-abuse problems. A few kids, like Andrea Zuckerman, do indeed steal into Beverly Hills even though they don't live there.

Some people could look at the characters on "Beverly, Hills 90210" and say, "How dare they have problems? They're too rich to have problems." First off, not everybody in Beverly Hills is filthy rich. The Walshes are like many in town who have just moderate means and must watch the budget. The family couldn't join the beach club because they couldn't afford it. They wanted to save for Brandon's and Brenda's college expenses.

Chuck Rosin remembers his teenage days driving to Beverly Hills High School "in a Chevy, not a Porsche. I don't think people watch 'Beverly Hills, 90210' and think, Boy, I can't wait to grow up and have that much money! This generation, maybe unlike kids in the eighties, is in a position to learn that business can boom and it can bust, too. We're not at all judgmental about money on this show. Material goods don't bring happiness, love, self-esteem, but we don't emphasize that lesson. We show things and let the audience judge for themselves. We take our viewers too seriously to spoon-feed them."

How does "Beverly Hills, 90210" manage to avoid wallowing in the wealth it depicts? By minimizing the role of adults who revel in materialism. "We show life in this community through the eyes of its young people," says Aaron Spelling. "If we cover drug abuse, we want to do it differently from every other show. In that episode, we had the mother addicted and we focused on the daughter's reaction. When we did the show about the Walsh parents not adjusting well to Beverly Hills and Mrs. Walsh meeting an old boyfriend, we concentrated on the kids' reaction. How did Brandon and Brenda feel? What's going to happen to them if their parents split up? Cancer—the same thing. It was Brenda's reaction that was the focus of that episode."

Series creator Darren Star is the first to credit John Hughes's influence on "Beverly Hills, 90210." Hughes is the writer-director-producer of such high school movies as *Sixteen Candles, Pretty in Pink, Some Kind of Wonderful, The Breakfast Club* and *Ferris Bueller's Day Off.*" Hughes likes to set up ordinary school situations like "who will take me to the prom?" or "why am I in detention?" and play them as seriously as grand opera. Teens in Hughes movies have emotions as strong as adults'. Their concerns are cosmic. They're real people feeling deeply.

"In his films, John Hughes has done what we're doing," Darren Star says. "Nobody else is doing it in TV."

Another kind of teen movie has attracted audiences in recent years—blacker, rougher, chancier. Call it the Deeper Rips School. Or the Christian Slater Movement. *Pump Up the Volume* and *Heathers* were hyper-hateful toward parents, super-scornful toward school.

Aaron Spelling acknowledges some influence from the Deeper Rips School. "Maybe we're a combination of that and Hughes," he says. "We're certainly not making one of those comedies where teenagers are presented as silly and awkward. We've got the humor of high school, and also the seriousness. I've learned from my daughter Tori that teens take life very, very seriously. If he calls to break a date, it's total rejection. If I can't make a friend right away, it's total rejection. If you don't live in the right part of town, and your friends notice, it's total rejection. Teenagers feel things in their lives with all their hearts. That level of emotion is what we're showing in 'Beverly Hills, 90210.'"

Where There's Emotion, Can Sex Be Far Away?

BRENDA: I like your butt—I mean your bike!
DYLAN: Thank you—hop on. My bike, that is.

"Beverly Hills, 90210" has nettled nervous Nellies because it dares to reflect the reality that 70 percent of seventeen-year-old girls have had sex. Accordingly, the majority of the show's characters aren't virgins. Even more revolutionary for television, the characters' sexual involvements haven't been presented as leaps off cliffs. Having sex didn't cause World War III. It was something people did—something important, but not the ultimate no-no, a crime for which punishment was certain.

Remember Brandon's first time, back in the show's fourth episode, when his old girlfriend came visiting from Minnesota? The operation was a success, and the patients survived. Brandon wore a condom, they expressed their deepest feelings, and they were happy afterward. Isn't that the way it should be?

Mr. and Mrs. Walsh, being parents, had to be worried. They had to be uncomfortable. Ultimately, though, they trusted Brandon, and they were right to trust him.

As it turned out, sex wasn't really the subject of that episode. The subject was the Minnesota girl's values and how a small dose of Beverly Hills could warp them. The episode placed sex in the context of the rest of life, where it belongs.

However, the show's critics really got steamed when Brenda's turn came in the first season's final episode, "Spring Dance." It could be that not very many adults were aware of the show when it first started airing. What they didn't know didn't hurt them. Or it could be that the old double standard is in operation—what's okay for Brandon isn't okay for Brenda.

The would-be censors' reaction to Brenda and

Dylan making love is even more surprising when you consider that the upshot of the episode was Brenda's decision to back off from sexual activity.

Here's Chuck Rosin's opinion: "The show has to be true to what fifteen- to nineteen-year-olds think. We're spotlighting that generation's likes and dislikes, their issues and concerns—not their parents'.

"Younger kids tune in and respond. They're interested in how high school kids act because they're going to be high schoolers themselves in a year or two. I think it was the parents of these younger kids who made noise about that Brenda-Dylan episode. Then they failed to look at the resolution of that story, when Brenda says she isn't ready, and it's too complicated for her right now.

"Isn't it more true to life to have a character try sex first before saying she's not ready for it? We're just portraying what goes on in life. We don't have an agenda, except to be true to the characters. We won't insult their intelligence.

"They used to talk about the MTV generation—the kids who wanted speed and flash and style. Well, this generation wants substance. We hear them say, 'My emotions are complicated.' Our show aims to entertain. That's why people tune in, to have fun. But they think, too. Without getting up on a soapbox—what a turnoff!—we give them something to think about, too."

As Darren Star says, "We won't be pulling back from sex. People wouldn't watch if we did. You can't run away from what's foremost on every teenager's mind."

Brandon Walsh is a character who has his romances but also makes his mistakes. When he goofs, he tries to set things right. He brings the values he's learned at home into his school, and he sticks to them. Jason Priestley walked in with the character. He had all the qualities we needed, plus the look our audience would like. Later on we found the depth of things he can play. He shows his soul in every scene he plays. There's really no limit to Jason Priestley.

—AARON SPELLING

Jason has all the heart and sensitivity of Brandon, but he's a much wilder guy. He's a freer spirit than the character. It's tough to play an interesting good guy, but Jason does it well. And on the set, he's the one who keeps everyone happy. He's got great energy to go with all that warmth.

—DARREN STAR

Actors who look good face a common stereotype: "He can't act." Jason, also known as the Franchise, contradicts that. You know Brandon is noble and true, but Jason shows his fallible side and keeps the character from being too righteous. Jason is always telling the writers, 'Loosen me up a little.' Jason is good at rewriting his dialogue to use youthful parlance. On the set, he's the guy who sets the tone of enthusiasm. He's the guys who makes the guest stars feel welcome.

—CHUCK ROSIN

Jason Priestley

EVERY SERIOUS TELEVISION ENSEMBLE drama has to have what program-makers call a *moral center*. He's the guy who defines the issues for the audience, makes the choices, learns the lessons.

Sometimes he's the most handsome guy in the cast, like Harry Hamlin on "L.A. Law." Other times he's not, like Daniel J. Travanti on "Hill Street Blues." On "Beverly Hills, 90210," he's blue-eyed Jason Priestley, and if he's not the handsomest, who is?

Brandon Walsh is often seen looking perplexed. His parents have given him a code to live by, but living by that code sometimes seems impossible in Beverly Hills. Brandon continually bends under the pressures of affluence and idleness, but he hasn't broken yet.

It's a challenge to play a character in such constant jeopardy from the fleshpots of Beverly Hills. But Jason Priestley is a pro, and he's found his own method of handling the barrage of story lines that keep putting him on the edge: he forgets. He puts down one script and picks up the next, and Brandon stays as naive as he needs to be.

Jason approaches his own burgeoning fame the same way: by forgetting that he's becoming famous. He still acts like one of the gang on the set of the show, slapping fives with the electricians, hugging Shannen Doherty, mock-boxing with Luke Perry, trading witticisms with Ian Ziering. He enjoys the same dumb "guy" pleasures he did before he hit it big: playing hockey, golfing, skiing, watching football on TV, gambling in Las Vegas, listening to Elvis Costello, jumping off bridges—that is, bungee jumping—elastic cord attached.

Before "Beverly Hills, 90210," Jason was an up-and-coming juvenile lead. Family shows on TV always require a ready stock of cute kids to portray the leading actors' children and make the stars look mature, kind, and sensitive. Most of the "Beverly Hills, 90210" cast has gone through this mill. Jason was doing very nicely as a juvenile lead on NBC's "Sister Kate," playing Stephanie Beacham's oldest orphan, when the chance to read for Aaron Spelling's new high school show came up.

To tell the story of his audition and spill the beans about most of what the world hungers to know about him, Jason chooses to talk in a deli about a mile away from the soundstage where the show's interiors are shot. He likes to keep publicity and acting separate. Another of Jason's rules: keep his family out of it.

He is all smiles and apologies as he arrives at Art's Deli ("Every sandwich a work of Art") half an hour late because work has detained him. He orders matzoh ball soup and a bagel with a pickle on the side and begins the Priestley saga: "'Sister Kate' had just wrapped for the season and we didn't know if it would be renewed. I got the 'Beverly Hills, 90210' script and asked who I had to read for. It was Aaron Spelling! Oh, great—just Aaron Spelling! I walked into his office, and the only thing I remember about it was how large the doorknobs were.

"Shannen Doherty was there. She had already been cast as Brenda, so I read my scene with her. They were down to the wire on choosing a Brandon. It was a Thursday, and shooting was supposed to start on the following Monday.

"My reading was good. I knew it was good. Afterward, Aaron looked up and down that big couch of his at all the other people sitting there. I guess they nodded. He said, 'Jason, can you find your way over to Fox?' I guess I could! I looked at my watch. I said, 'I think I could squeeze it in.' Everybody laughed, and I left.

"The reading for the people at Fox was the next day. That afternoon I got the word I was hired. It all happened very quickly."

"Sister Kate" could still have been renewed for another season, but Fox went with Priestley anyway. "They had to take a second position on my availability," Jason says. "Nobody could be sure that 'Sister Kate' wouldn't come back, and I was still obligated there.

"Obviously I prefer the way things worked out." Not necessarily because "Beverly Hills, 90210" made Jason a big star, either. "I prefer working on single-camera film, as on 'Beverly Hills, 90210,' to multi-camera video, which is the way 'Sister Kate' was shot, being a sitcom. Sitcoms are a strange hybrid mutant strain of theater and film. I'm glad I got the chance to do some sitcom work, but I like film. I prefer drama."

Before the "Beverly Hills, 90210" pilot went before the cameras on that Monday, the cast assembled at Aaron Spelling's house for a table reading and a get-together. The only cast member Jason knew was Shannen, and he only knew her from his brief audition a few days before. All of them sat around a big table drinking coffee and going through the script.

"It was nearly two years ago," Jason says, struggling to call up details of such ancient history. He tends to live as much as possible in the present, which is very healthy, but a by-product is a patchy memory.

"We were all a little timid at that first meeting, I think. Yeah, because a lot of us didn't know each other then. When I saw the others, I saw them as their characters. My first reaction to them was 'Wow, there was some really good casting here.' All the characters I'd read in the script were sitting around that table.

"I do remember one thing about that day. The director, Tim Hunter, and some of the producers got gift baskets, and so did all of us in the cast." Gift baskets are customary Hollywood perks. Floral arrangements also arrive on all occasions. "The baskets that Tim and the producer got had bottles of vodka, whiskey, whatever—but booze. All of us actors got baskets full of cookies and muffins. I remember complaining, 'Hey! I want one of the other kind of basket!'

"Oh, and I remember the coffee was good. And at one point I saw Tim standing in front of a painting on the wall, admiring it. I walked over and looked at it, too. It was a cool painting. Then I glanced down at the corner to see the signature. It was a Monet! Well, okaaaay!"

Aaron Spelling has produced more hours of prime time entertainment than anyone else, and he is not poor, not at all. "But the important thing about Aaron," Jason says, "is that he's a very sweet, sincere man, and that's why he's gone as far as he has."

Even though he's been playing Brandon now for a year and a half, Jason is reluctant to draw the inevitable comparisons between himself and his character. Most actors like to say that casting is the art of finding the similarities between the actor and the part, whereas the art of acting is finding the differences. Jason says, "I'm very different from Brandon. To play him, I found that little piece of Brandon within me. That piece of Brandon is inside everyone. It's that sliver of sincere morality in there. I found that piece in there, and enlarged it and brought it to the surface.

"Sincere morality—that's the trials and tribulations of trying to do the right thing and trying to be honest. Trying to be honest to others and to yourself. Really grappling with things that are morally incorrect. Maybe not always doing the right thing, but at least attempting to. It's the struggle that's important."

Brandon's struggle with the temptations of life in Beverly Hills is the core of the show. Brenda asks him, "Don't you ever get tired of always trying so hard to do the right thing?" The answer, of course, is "Yeah." Asked if he himself has encountered any of the kinds of moral dilemmas that Brandon is constantly faced with, Jason says, "We've all had moral conflicts. That's what makes life interesting. If there weren't any inner conflicts, we'd all be just the shells of humans, wouldn't we? I've had the usual conflicts everyone has had. Temptation is everywhere. You have to make the decision—you, not anyone else— whether you're going to give in to temptation. Your decision doesn't have anything to do with the devil or God or anything else. It's what feels right within you. Everyone has values, and everyone's values are different, and some stick to them more closely than others do."

What's been Brandon's strongest temptation so far? "The hardest thing was drinking. Teenagers drink. Who's kidding who? I drank when I was a teenager.

"But the pressures involved when you do are probably the most difficult that Brandon has faced so far. As he tells his parents after he's gone to jail, 'You don't know how much pressure there is.' Putting out information on that problem was probably the most beneficial thing the show could do. The message is that you don't have to drink just because the others are doing it. I had friends who died because of drinking and driving. I had friends who spent months in the hospital because of drinking and driving. I had friends who just totaled their car because of drinking and driving and luckily didn't hurt themselves or anybody else. So that drunk-driving episode has to be one of my favorites."

The show's pattern of Brandon overcoming temptation time and again could have bored viewers if Jason weren't a seasoned and astute actor. "Yeah, I guess it could become monotonous, if I let it," he said. "But I don't. That's an actor's job. My secret is that as soon as we finish one episode, I put the script down and I don't think about it anymore. I forget about it, and I move on to the next one. This morning, for instance, I was looping"—adding lines to the sound track after filming is finished—"and I hardly remembered the episode I was saying lines from.

"I go for immediacy, keeping it there in the present. That's how it stays fresh. If I can forget everything that's gone before, I can concentrate on the story I'm doing right now.

"In the beginning, Brandon was incredibly moralistic—maybe a little too moralistic. Now he's become a lot more fallible. Dylan tells him, 'Everybody has a dark side. You just hide it better than most.' Brandon has a lot more humor now. He's grown as a person in the last year. He sees the world more truthfully now, instead of seeing it only the way he wanted to see it. Before, he thought the world could be some kind of utopia. Maybe if everybody tried hard, everything could be great and wonderful. By now he realizes that all he can worry about effectively is his own little piece of the world, and try and make that as good as he can."

According to Jason, the change in Brandon is clear: "In the pilot, Brandon was in a Jacuzzi with a woman, and she suddenly suggested, 'Let's take off all our clothes.' Brandon said, 'Whoa, hey! Wait a minute,' thereby holding on to his strong moral fiber, trying to do the right thing by everybody. Today Brandon would be a little more relaxed about that. I can't pinpoint a single turning point. It's more subtle than that. I look back and see that's just the way he's grown."

Brandon does have more fun these days, and that's because Jason is such a fun-loving guy. "The show has a great balance of comedy and drama. Doing a show that was nothing but heavy drama would be boring, just as doing a show that was nothing but light comedy would be trivial. The show is like real life, which has lighter moments and heavier moments. The writers do a good job creating lighter scenes.

"Sometimes the cast members throw in little gags. I remember one day I was walking down the street in Hollywood. Ian Ziering pulled up next to me in his car. I said, 'What's going on, Eye?' He was trying to find someplace that sold X-ray gogs—you know, special goggles, the kind of thing you order from ads in the back of comic books. 'Get me a pair, too,' I yelled at him. We ended up using them on the show, the Spring Dance episode, for looking at the girls."

Jason's manner during shooting is unique. He helps keep everyone, cast and crew, relaxed with a continual stream of banter, but there's no sleeping or lollygagging on the set when Jason is around. Shannen Doherty has caught Jason's act: "Yes, it's a big running joke around here. Jason will say, 'Hey, let's go!' and everybody else will groan and say, 'Yeah, right. Take a break, Jason!'"

Jason says of his breezy working style: "Yeah, I try to be that way. It creates a lighter atmosphere, which is good to have, even when we're doing really heavy scenes. If you can keep everybody up and happy, we'll do better work. I do like to move things along. Sometimes it gets a little slow. I did once ride my motorcycle down the hallway when the girls were doing a really slow scene. It was pretty funny.

"We're all friends. We all get along better than you might expect with a show where most of the cast is in the same age range. We're lucky, I guess. We're just people who get along. There isn't the little competitive baloney and bickering you hear about so much on some shows. So-and-so feuding with the producer—we don't have that. There's nothing worse than a battle of the egos on a set. Instead of that, we're all real supportive of each other. I think it comes across on the screen, don't you?"

Jason maintains as normal an off-camera life as possible. He says, "The guys I hang out with most are Luke and Ian. The three of us are around the same age, and we share similar interests. What do we do together? We do stupid guy things. We spend many a Sunday at my house watching football on TV. Guy stuff.

"Luke and I, we took Ian to the Charlton Heston Celebrity Shoot. So now Eye's hooked on guns. Luke and I go bungee jumping together, and Ian's coming with us next time. He's made a big point of that. I love it when you're standing on the bridge getting ready to jump off. People have died bungee jumping, but you try not to think about that.

"It's an amazing sensation to willingly commit suicide—to jump off a high bridge—because you forget you have this secure cord attached to you. You commit yourself and you jump off and all you feel is utter terror. You've killed yourself! It's all over! Then you're yanked back up by the cord, and you feel complete euphoria. There are no words to describe it.

"The time I feel most alive is when I come closest to death. That moment when you bounce back up is so amazing. Amazing! You feel so alive! 'I'm still here!' you're thinking. 'I'm just swinging here!'

"Now I can't wait to try skydiving. That's gotta be a cool feeling, to jump out of a perfectly good airplane. When you do things like that, you don't think about the danger; you just want to do it. Bungee jumping gives you a ground rush. You're only two hundred fifty feet up off the ground and you can see what you could be jumping onto if you weren't attached. Skydiving, you're fifteen thousand feet up in the air, and the ground looks like a quilt, so it's gotta be a different sensation."

Jason is an all-around sportsman, but he isn't as active as he used to be. "No rugby anymore. I still play hockey. You grow up in Canada, hockey is what you play. It's a great sport. It makes the producers of 'Beverly Hills, 90210' a little nervous when I play. They wanted me to quit hockey, wanted to put it in my contract, but I said I wouldn't give it up. They tried to stop me from riding my motorcycle, too, but that didn't happen, either. I can't say I blame 'em for trying, but no way!

"As a kid I wanted to be as good a hockey player as I could be. My play did reach a certain level, but I realized I just wasn't good enough to go farther. We didn't have a school team. I played rep hockey, meaning I played on the team that represented our district, South Delta, where I lived, in Vancouver. If you play rep, you're one of the better players."

Now, as an adult, Jason has played in the Los Angeles County Hockey Association, which he pronounces "Lotcha." "I played last summer and winter. But I missed the league this summer, and something tells me I'm not going to play this winter, either. It isn't fair to the other guys on the team when you keep on not showing up because of your job.

"There are some really good players. Ninety percent of the guys are from Canada or the Northeast, and they grew up on skates. It's very competitive. I play center, which can be the glory position, but not for me. I'm not the glory guy.

"I play on the Celebrity All-Stars, playing left wing. We travel around the country and play six or eight matches a year in different cities, raising money for local charities. We've raised over two million dollars so far. Matt Frewer plays, and a lot of other Canadians. This will be my third season on the team."

Fans of Jason's hockey prowess got a chance to see his skillful skate work in the episode last summer when he was the Big Brother of an abused child. Jason roller-bladed swiftly down the bike path that follows the Pacific shoreline of Los Angeles. Most stars have to use stuntmen for scenes like that one.

Sports and acting were always parallel ambitions for Jason. The balance tilted acting's way when he was a teenager and realized that he would never grow past average height no matter how good he was.

He thought about acting early, he recalls: "I told my Mom when I was five that's what I wanted to do. She said, 'Okay, but that means you'll have to take a bath every day.' 'Wait a minute,' I said, 'I'll have to think about this again!'"

Jason prefers short, indirect answers to questions that touch on his personal life. Although he once talked to teen magazines about the type of girls he likes, and so forth, he now realizes that his future lies in creating awareness of himself as an adult. He downplays his good looks, joking that in about five years he'll wake up and see the craggy face of Jeremy Irons in the mirror.

Ask him about his life when he was growing up as an actor-athlete and Jason will laugh the question off. His home situation "didn't resemble Brandon's in the slightest. It was different in every way, shape, and form. To start with, I had a lot more snow and rain when I was growing up.

"But I don't want to talk about my upbringing. I don't like to talk about my parents. I love them very much. They lead their lives, and their lives are their own business. What they do is up to them. I respect their privacy.

"Let me quote the immortal Yul Brynner here: 'The facts of my life have nothing to do with the realities of my present.'

"I don't remember much about my childhood, anyway. I guess I'll have to go through some of that regressive therapy so I can go back to the womb." A few of the facts of Jason's life that have filtered through: he has an older sister who lives in London; his mother is now a real estate agent; his father is a manufacturer's representative for a furniture and textile company.

Sitting in Art's Deli on Ventura Boulevard in Los Angeles, Jason racks his memory to come up with a reason why he chose his life's work while he still had his baby teeth. To help himself think, he dunks his pickle in his soup. "Why did I decide to be an actor? That's a tough one. I guess I thought it looked like fun. I watched TV and thought I could do it, too."

When Jason told his mom about his ambitions, it wasn't an idea that came totally out of the blue. Mrs.

Priestley, whose father was a circus acrobat, was a dancer, singer, choreographer, and teacher. She had an agent and thus was able to point her son in the right direction. "I think she was teaching at the time," Jason remembers. "I was fortunate that my mother knew how to facilitate my desire to be an actor. It wasn't simple. Nothing is ever easy. But it happened. I worked with a certain frequency. I was very lucky that I got to work a lot and learn a lot from being around adults at work."

Jason also counts himself lucky that he was able to learn his trade in the provincial media, far from the brightest lights a thousand miles to the south. He says, "I was a child actor in Vancouver, not a child actor in Los Angeles. So I didn't have all the pressures that kids who work here have. There were only three or four kids like me, so there wasn't all this insane competition. There was enough work to go around, and we all just did it and didn't have to think about it too much."

Jason downplays the importance of his early acting work: "I did a lot of fruit juice ads. Luncheon meat. Kid things. None of the commercials were on in America, just Canada. My first big dramatic role was when I was eight and I played the son of a woman who was crazy. I don't remember if I thought that was some big step for me. I think I did know it was something more important than commercials. It was 'Stacey,' for the Canadian Broadcasting Company. It was a pretty big part. I got to do a crying scene. I got to do some fun stuff, like riding around in a go-cart.

"That was back in the days before the child labor laws. I got to work fourteen hours a day, along with everybody else. I never thought about being tired or anything. I do remember one day we were filming late. I was going to go night skiing on Grouse Mountain. From the location where we were filming you could see the mountain, with the trails all lit up. I wasn't tired at all. 'When are we going to be done?' I just couldn't wait to ski. Never did get to it that night. I wish I had that energy now. In a few years I'll be up to forty cups of coffee a day.

"I got all the money I earned, and I spent it on candy and stuff. What did I care? Money was never a motivating factor for me, and it still isn't. There have been times when I was broke and I was starving, and I needed to earn something. But most of the time I've had a job and I've been paid. I've never lost sight of the fact that acting is a job, just a job.

"It's also a passion, of course. It's something you really have to care about, or else you can't do it. Or if you did it just for the money, what's the point? People can tell if money is your only motivation."

Since he didn't need the money, young Jason got out of the business as soon as it started getting in the way of his fun. "I worked quite a bit until I was about thirteen, when I quit," he says. "I didn't want to have to worry about my face getting cut. It isn't a healthy way for a kid to grow up, always being worried that you might get hurt, and what if I have an audition tomorrow? I never did worry about that. I did everything with complete and utter reckless abandon, like kids are supposed to. I didn't want to even have to think about jeopardizing my acting career, so I quit acting!"

As a "normal" teenager with no image to preserve, Jason had all of the hair cut off the sides of his head and sported a modified Mohawk. He wore chains, black jeans, and combat boots—a far cry from the plaid-shirted Brandon!

"Then," he recalls, "I picked up acting again after I got out of high school. I came back to acting because I missed it. When I started thinking about what I wanted to do with my life, I found out I had a passion for it. I really loved it. I hadn't done it for a few years, but I still had a real craving to do it. The fact that the desire to do it stayed with me for that whole time was a pretty good indication that it was the thing I truly wanted to do. I'd messed around with acting in school, community theater stuff in eleventh and twelfth grades. I really loved doing theater."

When he decided to work toward a career as an actor, Jason took himself seriously enough to study with June Whitaker. She had been a founding member of the Neighborhood Playhouse in New York and had moved to Vancouver. Jason studied with her for about two years and found a few professional jobs. One 1986 assignment was in a Marlo Thomas TV movie, *Nobody's Child,* which was shot in Vancouver. Jason's tiny part was called Second Boy.

"One of the funnest things I did back then was cowrite, coproduce, edit, score, and star in a short film called *One Single Raindrop* with a friend of mine named Steve Cooper. It was probably one of the greatest learning experiences I've ever had, to take a project from the germination of an idea all the way to the finished product. It was eight or nine minutes long. It was about two best friends. One of them got killed, and how the other one dealt with it. It was shown on a cable channel in Canada. It's bizarre and maybe a little esoteric for most people.

"Then I came to L.A. in 1987 and started doing what we do here." What they do in Los Angeles is go to meetings, read for parts, audition, and test for parts—and nine times out of ten, lose the parts. Jason caught on more quickly than most. He did a TV movie, *Lies from Lotusland.* In Los Angeles and Vancouver, he has appeared on episodes of "21 Jump Street," "Quantum Leap," "McGyver," "Airwolf" and others. He starred in the Disney Channel's "Teen Angel" and "Teen Angel Returns." Most important, he won the role of Todd Mahaffey on "Sister Kate." That part gave him the week-after-week visibility that made him the prime contender for the male lead in "Beverly Hills, 90210."

Jason was always a fun-loving guy, and now that the world is beating a path to his door, he's the same fun-loving guy. Shooting "Beverly Hills, 90210" could be a tedious treadmill of long hours and short tempers. It's happened on other shows with casts full of ambitious up-and-comers. Jason is the actor largely responsible for the positive energy everyone feels pulsing around the "Beverly Hills, 90210" set. The show's producers call him "the Franchise" not just because his character is the moral center of the show but because Jason himself is the acknowledged leader of the cast.

As Gabrielle Carteris says, "Jason is very bright. He's there for you if you need him if you're having a bad day. He's got the strongest desire of any of us to direct. He's always talking to the crew about technical stuff."

"When I work, I try to have a good time on the set," Jason says, laboring to put into words the philosophy he brings to his job. "Acting should be fun. That's why I became an actor—because it looked like fun. Sure, there are times when you're doing a really heavy scene, you're not having fun. On some other shows, there's no fun even during the lighter scenes. On ours, because there's no bickering and stuff, everyone can have a good time during the light scenes. And during the heavy scenes everyone knows the difference, and they're all behind you.

"The show is a team effort. If the actors and crew all work together and there's no big separation between us, that's the way it should be, I think. Then again . . . who the hell am I? I might be wrong. I probably am, and it wouldn't be the first time.

"When I go in and I have to do a big scene, I know the crew will support me. If I have to go off and be alone to work on a scene I've got to do, everyone understands. They know it's no big deal; it's just Jason doing his work. 'Jay, go do what you gotta do.'

"Sometimes scenes require work; sometimes they don't. It depends on the particular scene and on how well I'm flowing that day, how my emotions are behaving. Most of the time, though, I don't need to take that moment. I just do it. People visit the set and see me work and ask me how I can joke and mess around and then snap right into some dramatic moment. I tell them I have no problem doing that. I trained and I studied acting for a long time. I've gotten to the point where I'm comfortable with the character. I can turn Brandon on and off very easily."

In creating Brenda, I remembered my own sister. She's a year younger than me and she went through high school with me back in suburban Maryland. Shannen is much more mature than Brenda, and very intelligent. When I talk to Shannen, I feel like I'm talking to someone who's older than a teenager. She's very independent. She's passionate about her acting—in fact, she's passionate about whatever she's doing at any given moment. And she's really expressive. That's what makes teenage girls in the audience identify so closely with her.

—DARREN STAR

Shannen's so passionate! In dramatic moments she generates a lot of power. At first Brenda didn't have much humor, but when we brought that in, Shannen played it to the hilt. She's a total pro.

—CHUCK ROSIN

We knew from *Heathers* that Shannen was a very good actress. We wondered if she could show naïveté. We tested her, and she showed everything and made it look easy. She's marvelous at the what-am-I-doing-in-a-strange-city vulnerability. Where Shannen gets to me—she's a marvelous reactor. Reacting is the essence of acting, and she knows how to make reaction shots count. Also, she's the best crier I've ever seen. Shannen could cry at a jai alai match.

—AARON SPELLING

Shannen Doherty

SHANNEN HAS HAD SUCCESS WRITTEN ALL over her from an early age. She was always focused straight ahead, and she has consistently struck her coworkers as determined, knowledgeable, and competent.

Although anyone can see at a glance that she's stunningly beautiful, she's never been one to coast on her looks. Other pretty girls waited for things to come to them; Shannen reached out and grabbed the goodies.

Oddly, she isn't quite convinced that she's beautiful. She's like Brenda, who, when her mother calls her beautiful, answers, "Not California beautiful." Shannen's word for herself is "unusual-looking." True, but the word should be "unusually good." She has a killer smile and a fresh, clear complexion, but her best feature is her eyes. They instantly tell the truth about her feelings. They can bore in like lasers when she's angry, or they can light up broadly when something strikes her funny.

On the set of "Beverly Hills, 90210," she's one of the quieter, more serious ones. One reason is that her character has to be that way. Being in love with Dylan is no laughing matter! Another, though, is Shannen's professional attitude. She keeps her eyes on the prize.

She vigorously pursued the part of Brenda and endured some well-founded worries about whether she would ever get to play the part. She describes her auditioning experience: "When I first read the 'Beverly Hills, 90210' script, I knew I was perfect for the part, and I think most of the producers felt that way, too. Things like that, you just know. You just have a gut feeling about it.

"First I met the casting directors, who knew my work, so I didn't have to read a scene for them. My first reading was for Aaron Spelling and the other producers. Aaron supported me, and so I took the next step and went to Fox. I read for the network once, and then they flew a girl in from New York and it was between the two of us. We both read for Fox again and afterward I knew I'd blown it. Oh, God, I did so bad! I was really bummed because this show was the best pilot I'd read, the one with the most substance, and I really wanted to be a part of it. I told one of the casting directors how bad I felt, how I wasn't going to get it, and he winked at me and said, 'Yes, you will—trust me.'

"I did get it, of course, but then the whole thing was that they couldn't find someone to play Brandon. I had my part, but I might lose the job anyway. They were going to dump the show before it went into production if they couldn't find an actor they liked to play Brandon. I really hoped we'd find a guy! There were five to pick from. I read with all five of them, and Jason got the part the next day.

"From what I heard, I was seen for the show because Tori Spelling had seen me in the movies in *Heathers* and on TV in 'Our House.' The producers had seen a whole group of girls before me. They were worrying about filling the part of Brenda, and they didn't know who they wanted, when Tori went to her dad and suggested me. So I owe part of it to Tori."

Shannen brought a lot to the party. She's been a professional for half of her twenty years, working in commercials, voice-overs, episodic television, TV movies, and feature films. Much of her work involved being somebody's daughter, so she was primed to star in a series where she was the somebody and another actress played the secondary role of somebody's mother.

She was born in Memphis and moved with her parents to Los Angeles when she was six and her older brother Sean was ten. Four years later Shannen became interested in acting and joined a children's theater group. This led to finding an agent and getting auditions. Her first part was in a Michael Landon production, a two-part episode of "Father Murphy," playing a character named Drucilla

Shannen. It was a lucky name—not just the "Shannen" part, but also "Drucilla," which just happened to be the name of Shannen's doll.

Even then, Shannen knew how to be all business. Michael Landon commented: "You could see that she treated this as a business. It was not a case of a parent wanting a show-business career for a child, which is often the case." Shannen went on to win roles in Landon's "Little House: A New Beginning," in which she played Melissa Gilbert's best friend during the show's last season, 1982-83. Later, Landon used her in an episode of "Highway to Heaven." She guest-starred in many other series of the day, including "Airwolf."

Most of Shannen's career as a preteen was in commercials and documentaries. One important job was providing the voice of a very responsible child mouse in the 1982 animated feature *The Secret of NIMH.* Another was in *Night Shift,* also in 1982, playing a tiny role along with such other future notables as Shelley Long and Kevin Costner. A third feature credit was *Girls Just Want to Have Fun,* in 1985. Her TV movie credits included the role of Lindsay Wagner's daughter in *The Other Lover* in 1985 and the part of Brad Davis's daughter in *Robert Kennedy and His Times* the same year (Jason Bateman from "Valerie" played her brother!).

Her big break came in 1986 when she was cast as the goal-oriented, shoulders-back Kris Witherspoon in "Our House." Shannen used to get bags and bags of mail from kids seeking advice, figuring that Kris was so together that Shannen must know everything. As young as she was, Shannen was already sticking up for herself on the set of the show. Shannen also worked to keep Kris as virtuous as she always appeared on screen. At one point she requested that the producers cut a line Kris was supposed to say mentioning condoms, because it made her uncomfortable. Perky Kris was bound and determined to go to the Air Force Academy, but the series ran only two years and she never reached her goal.

After "Our House" was canceled, Shannen won the eye-catching part of Heather Duke in the teen cult film *Heathers,* which came out in 1989. This Heather was no Brenda! She was Winona Ryder's principal antagonist in the film, a young lady determined to freeze out anyone who didn't meet the Heathers' high standards of bitchiness.

Meanwhile, Shannen was coming in to work every day with her mother, Rosa, who remained on the set with her all day. Her father Tom, a stroke victim and a diabetic, was also a frequent visitor. Shannen was of two minds about school. She wanted to go to regular schools, but her work often interfered. She did attend in ninth and twelfth grades. The rest of the time she endured the studio school.

She recalls that period of her life and its effect on her ability to play Brenda: "Things that had happened in my own life helped me understand what Brenda was going through. For instance, in the pilot Brenda dates an older guy. I did the same thing when I was a freshman in high school. Actually I didn't lie about my age to him, as Brenda did in the show. It was more that I never introduced him to my parents. And I was like Brenda in that I also switched schools a couple of times. So I knew what it was like to come from somewhere else and want badly to be accepted by a new group.

"I've always tended to date older guys—until now, until my present boyfriend. I think a lot of teenage girls date boys older than them. In my case, I've been working as an actress for eleven years. I grew up faster than your normal teenager. I've always been very business-aware, very ambitious and goal-oriented. I've never understood people who didn't have any future plans or weren't striving for something in their lives. That's why I never dated high school guys when I was in high school—I clearly didn't understand them! I knew what I wanted to do with my life. I'm not saying it should be that way for everyone, but for me it was easier to date guys who were older, who already had a career. They'd understand if my work made me cancel a date or something.

"Now it's all different. I'm just discovering with my boyfriend that the great thing about dating someone closer to your own age is that you can grow together and learn about relationships together. If the guy is too much older than you, he could be jaded, and when something happens, he's already seen it and he knows how it's going to go.

"I didn't tell my parents about the older boy I was dating because I didn't think they would understand. Eventually, when dating older boys became a constant thing, I decided to be honest about it, and I found out that they did understand. Don't get me wrong, the guys weren't in their forties or something ancient like that. Close, though!

"The older I've gotten, the more my parents have turned into my friends, people I trust and can tell anything to. They've always been big on the parent-daughter thing—being close, being able to open up to your family. I was raised that way, but when I was first dating this older guy, I just couldn't imagine that my parents had ever gone through the things I was going through. They never did this! I thought. Them? No way! Of course, they had. You tell your mom, you make this big confession, and she says, 'Oh, honey, I did that, too, when I was your age.' You go, 'What?'"

Remembering her days as a teen trying to fit in, Shannen says, "When I would transfer schools, the new school would always have these cliques. It was always hard to break in to a tight group like that. The whole point of cliques is to keep outsiders out. Also, being the new girl, I had a different life-style from the others at my schools. I'm from Memphis, Tennessee. I dressed differently; I had a different look. I lacked the classic look of the basic blond tanned California girl. I was dark haired, very white-skinned, and unusual-looking. No one would say I looked pretty. I don't blend into the crowd. You're always striving to make it, to be the cool person in school. I had my acting work, and the others were always going out and having fun.

"Eventually I just decided, the hell with it. Forget it! I don't need this! If people want to be my friends, it'll be because of who I am, not what I look like or the way I dress. That's when I began to make friends! Because I was myself. It's the same kind of thinking that Brenda went through, though I didn't feel I had to go to the extreme of being tempted to shoplift in order to own the right clothes. Brenda soon realized that she didn't need to do anything besides be herself. She was who she was. Plus, when Dylan came into the picture, that raised her confidence level—a lot! She's dating the coolest guy in school? The one that all the girls wanted. Instantly she became cool, too. Even if she wasn't typical-looking or pretty, she got the cool guy."

Talking about how a girl's "cool" rating can depend on how cool her boyfriend is, Shannen says, "I didn't have many boyfriends when I was in high school, and none of them were from the school, or even in high school. People thought I must be weird. Once everyone found out about who I was dating and found out that he was in college, the cooler I seemed. They all wanted to meet his college friends!

"Once Brenda started going out with Dylan, she started depending on him a lot, and maybe they rushed things in their relationship. Maybe she jumped into things too fast. She had to backpedal, and they had to break up. 'I'm not used to these feelings,' she says. Brenda found out that you don't need to have a boyfriend to be accepted or to like yourself. And that's a good lesson for teenagers watching the show. You always think that if you can get a boyfriend, wow! you'll be accepted."

Plus, there was conflict at home over Dylan. Mr.

Walsh will never approve of someone like Dylan for his baby girl. The tension over the dinner table gives sweet Brenda a chance to spit some real venom: "Thanks for dinner! It's been real."

"After Brenda broke up with Dylan, she found she could be happy just in who she was. She'd been thinking about dropping out of school and moving out. Now she's really evolved as a person. She's back together with Dylan, but it's a whole new relationship. She's more comfortable, more confident. She's secure about how fast things should go. The way things have turned out, the show has presented a lot of different aspects of a relationship in high school.

"Brenda pulled back because of the too-much-too-soon thing. That happens. They'd been dating four months before they had sex. Then she got scared about whether she was pregnant. 'Maybe I rushed into this. Maybe I didn't think it through.' She became aware of her responsibilities. Responsibility about birth control, sexually transmitted diseases, AIDS. There's an emotional responsibility, too. Brenda is one who wants to really commit to a person first. She wants to be sure she's in love with him. She wouldn't want sex to be the only thing in a relationship. She had to slow down and evaluate her feelings and decide if she was ready for that intense a relationship."

Will sex rear its head again? Can Dylan and Brenda restrain themselves, and what might be the consequences if they don't? "I would think sex will come up again," Shannen says. "Once you're sexually active, you can't be a virgin again. I'm sure the question will come up again, whether she says yes or no—it's inevitable. Especially since the boy is Dylan, who seems somewhat mature in that department, fairly sexually active!

"I think she's truly in love with him, and he is truly in love with her—even though they're awfully young. She's sixteen and he's seventeen, I'd say. But that's not uncommon at all. I have friends who were high school sweethearts, and now five years later they're still together. Love is powerful, isn't it? One thing, though—the show could get a little stale, with Brenda and Dylan staying in this relationship, if there aren't any outside influences."

As for Brenda's friendship with Kelly, Brenda began insecurely and now has become Kelly's equal. Shannen describes the relationship: "In the pilot, Kelly made the first move to be friends with Brenda. For Brenda, it was, God, this cool girl is talking to me! You always want to hang around with the cool people. On the outside, Kelly can seem snobby and bitchy. Inside, she's actually a kindhearted, good person. By now, between Brenda and Kelly there's a true bond that girlfriends can have. Kelly has confessed her mother's cocaine and alcohol problems, and that has bonded Brenda to her. It's a bond that's very hard to sever."

Shannen takes life seriously, and she's pleased that "Beverly Hills, 90210" goes so deeply into issues. "My favorite episodes were the ones about breast cancer and date rape and AIDS," she says. "The writers handled those issues wonderfully. After Brenda had her mammogram, and when they operated and found out the growth was benign, I got a lot of mail from viewers. Breast cancer isn't a huge problem in high school, but it is something you should take into consideration.

"The people who wrote me about it said that they test themselves regularly now. One girl who wrote said she'd gone through the exact same thing Brenda did. 'Now that Brenda is okay, I know I'll be okay,' she wrote. I loved being able to give that girl positive thoughts. 'Beverly Hills, 90210' has a big responsibility to send out the right messages. If the show can help one person, we've achieved our goal.

"I like the episodes that deal with issues. Date rape is such a big problem, and it's ignored a lot. When we went into date rape, we didn't gloss over anything. We don't always have to have a happy ending to each episode. All the characters get their chance to mess up. It's very true to life. The drunk-driving episode, for instance, where Brandon gets thrown into jail. And I also liked the episode about Kelly and her mom's alcoholism, which showed the other side. It showed that older people can have big problems, too, and teenagers sometimes have to help the adults get through them."

Perhaps because Shannen has been so prominently in the public eye for so long, she has developed a healthy reserve when it comes to the media. More than most, she has been burned by publications that misrepresent her forthrightness. Shannen gets an endorsement from Gabrielle Carteris: "Shannen and I work really well together. If a child comes on the set, she'll just take that child under her wing. She's a nurturer, and she'll direct some day."

Shannen says, "The people in the cast all like each other. Obviously we do read all the things about ourselves in the supermarket papers, taking potshots at us and following us around and trying to put us in compromising positions. When you're in the public eye, you can't help but make a mistake once in a while, but it shouldn't be exaggerated the way those publications do. It's very reassuring to come back to the set after something like that and get reassured by the other actors.

"Jason, in particular, is a great guy and easy to get along with. We adore each other. Jason is a guy I can go to with my personal problems. He gives me great advice. We trust each other, so we can give our opinions honestly, and we can joke around. If things get a little stressful on the set and I get a little on edge, I can go into Jason's dressing room, and his music is blasting, and I can mellow out. We've come to rely on each other. We all help pull each other through the days. We can relax and do the job. When you work together for fourteen-hour days, it helps to get along. We've all adjusted to each other's personality now, and we're all much closer on the second season. There's no star of this show, there's an ensemble, and we all treat each other as equals.

"I'm also real close to the girls who do my make-up and hair, Cherie and Doreen. I won't do anything without them now. I won't do a photo shoot without them. That's how good they are. They're so support-ive."

Turning to Luke Perry, the man she spends the

most quality time with on screen, Shannen says, "Luke is a double-sided guy. He's quiet, and he's not. He's a guy you have to get to know to understand. I've had plenty of time to get to know him. You have to learn that you can't take what he says too seriously. Otherwise you'll be offended. After a while he and I learned each other's sense of humor. I've learned how he jokes, and by now he knows my very dry sense of humor. A lot of people don't know when I'm joking. Now none of us take any of the others seriously! We laugh constantly. I love it when he and Jason do something like pull down their pants and show their boxers in the middle of a shot, which they did one time and made me laugh my head off for about ten minutes.

"None of us like tension on the set. It'll show up on camera. So we'll do whatever we can to get rid of it. Luke and Jason are the chief pranksters. When the fourteenth or even the fifteenth hour of the workday rolls around, you've got to be joking. You're giddy with fatigue. But then you have to look at it in perspective. Here we are, forced to spend hour after hour, day after day, working with these horrendous-looking, ugly, dull guys. It's a really tough job, you know. And the guys—no wonder they're so grumpy, having to work with a bunch of hags like us!"

Shannen is passing on her feelings about the show during a lunch break from shooting exterior scenes at the real school, Torrance High, that stands in for West Beverly. For her break, she has changed out of her well-tailored Brenda costume into lounge-around Shannen clothes, slacks and a blouse. She's sitting in the middle of a grass playing field while the rest of the cast and crew are chowing down.

Looming in the grass nearby is shirtless Luke Perry, with a look of yearning on his face. There's something lacking in his life, something major-major. It's a cigarette, and Shannen's got some. She supplies Luke's urge, and he stays and joins the conversation.

"Shannen and I were thrust into this together," he says. "Wham! You guys are in love!"

Shannen adds: "We'd barely met, and we had to kiss each other and work really . . . closely."

"There were times—I'll be real honest—when we saw things differently. To put it nicely."

Shannen laughs—a long-running giggle.

Luke turns serious: "I believe that it stemmed from us both being very sure of what we wanted to do and how to do it. We just have different ways of going about it."

"We're both perfectionists," Shannen admits. "In that situation, sometimes you're not the most mellow person in the world. This year we all get along."

"Last year we had something to prove, as a group," says Luke. "There was a lot of stress."

Shannen agrees: "Yeah, we all felt that. And plus, last year, a lot of the show was on Jason and me."

"This year, the load is spread out," Luke says. "Used to be, these two guys were in the first shot and the last shot every day."

"Now, the pressure's off. Now Luke and I don't

even mind kissing each other once in a while, do we?"

"Watch!" Luke gives Shannen a brotherly kiss on the lips that shades into something a little less platonic, then saunters off.

Shannen continues, "The show has such a great cast; it should have been more about the ensemble from the beginning. But they were trying to build the show, so the audience needed to focus on Brenda and Brandon while they were establishing what the show was about. Now it's definitely an ensemble. The bonus is that we don't have to work quite such long hours and it's an easier-going set.

"This year we have more of the 'thirtysomething' concept, where one episode leads into another. I think the show is definitely better this year. I just hope we don't stray away from controversial issues. If you're popular, you can fall into being just the hip show of the moment and lose what you started out to do. But so far we haven't done that. We've got a show on racism coming up, and we'll cover some other heavy things, too."

Shannen's personal future surely involves major stardom, no matter how long "Beverly Hills, 90210" runs. Look for her to use her next hiatus from the show in 1992 to star in a strong TV movie or feature film. One day, she vows, she will direct. When you think of Shannen, think Katharine Hepburn, think Meryl Streep.

Dylan is a kid on the edge, trailing a sense of danger behind him. Which way will he go? Will he get Brandon in trouble or will he become a friend? Luke Perry delivered in spades. Actually, Luke's a real fun guy to be around. He and Jason are like the Bobbsey Twins together—they're nonstop uppers. They play scenes together, and I have to look twice to see if the camera is running, it's so much like real life.

—AARON SPELLING

Stardom agrees with Luke Perry. It's been terrific to see his growth over the last year. He's really effective in projecting the character's air of mystery. He's such an intense actor, even after you've read the script you never quite sure how he'll play the scene. All those troubles, all that vulnerability, yet Luke is a real live-wire character on the set.

—CHUCK ROSIN

Luke has a lot of the qualities you see in Dylan. He's intense; he's complex. In addition, Dylan is a morally centered guy, and Luke is the same way. Luke thinks a lot—though he's not a tortured guy like Dylan. You see Dylan off camera, there's still an air of intrigue about him. It's not some wall. It's a seductive quality, and warm.

—DARREN STAR

Luke Perry

WHY DOES LUKE PERRY ATTRACT THE MOST
fan mail of any "Beverly Hills, 90210" star? His part
isn't the biggest, but Dylan McKay has a wounded-
puppy quality. He's handsome as the devil, but he
doesn't seem to know it. He's cool to be kind. He's
been around and sometimes seems a thousand years
old. Dylan is one of those tormented creatures who
rouse the mothering and loving instincts in most
female viewers, without scaring off the young men
watching.

Luke himself has a past, and he's quite frank in
disclosing his checkered career in school back in
Ohio. Now far beyond that schoolboy rebellion, he's
grown into a level-headed young man with plenty of
reserves to handle all the attention he's getting.

Sitting unpretentiously in a pigeon-poop speck-
led outside stairwell of Torrance High, the location
"Beverly Hills, 90210" uses for school scene exteriors, Luke tells his story in a voice as light and feath-
ery as Clint Eastwood's. Watch out for his sense of
humor: it's dry, and it hides between the lines.

Luke was in a slow phase of his career—working
a day job, in fact, when he was summoned to meet
the "Beverly Hills, 90210" casting directors and producers. "I was working for a construction company,
estimating and bidding on jobs," he says, "when I got
the call from my agent to read for this part. It wasn't
the kind of job you can just walk off to go audition. I
made up some blatant lie to get away.

"I wasn't wearing a shirt at work. I was all
sweaty. So, I borrowed an old shirt out of the trunk
of my friend's car. It had oil spots all over it and no
buttons. I tied it on, I walked in and I grabbed the
sides"—sheets of paper containing his audition
scene. "One of the lines my character had was 'I'm
not in a very good mood today.' So, as it happened, I
didn't have to act much to say that.

"I got called back for another reading. I gave the
construction company another heinous lie. I kept
getting not rejected. I had to come and read for
Aaron Spelling. I don't remember anything about my
reading. They told me about it later. They said I
slouched into his office like I owned the place.
According to them, I put my feet up on his table. I lit
up a cigarette without asking permission and started
to talk. I don't think in my right mind I'd ever do
that, do you? I guess I did do it, though.

"After I read for the network powers that be, the powers that be at Fox were not so hot on yours truly. They wanted to go another way. Mr. Spelling, however, went to the mat for me, and here I am. I don't know what they were looking for, but they didn't want to keep me after my first episode. It was supposed to be a one-shot deal. Then Mr. Spelling looked at the dailies of my scenes and said, 'Let's keep him around.'

"Mr. Spelling is a good friend to have. I was always very respectful of the man, but now that I know the man, I'm even more so. He was the producer of 'Starsky and Hutch,' which was my favorite show growing up."

What made Aaron Spelling retain Luke? Luke not only exuded telegenic magnetism but also, showed that he'd done a lot of thinking about Dylan. He recalls, "I was real sure I didn't want to play a high school hoodlum with a bad attitude. They created an interesting background for Dylan, so he had lots of interesting ways to go. I decided he had to be brilliant. Not that he'd go around spouting brilliant things all day. Brilliant inside. Inside, he's contemplative. His thought processes are very fast. It looks like he does things on impulse? Nooooo. They're totally thought through. I figure he's an intellectual first and everything else second. Plus, he's got a lot of problems, and problems make for good drama and make characters interesting to play."

If Dylan's so smart, why does he go to school at all? "I thought about that a lot. He goes as a self-protective measure. He knows enough about himself to realize that if he stays away from school, the other side of him might get pretty dark. Even though he's not afraid of the dark, there's no sense in tempting fate. Nine-tenths of the reason he's still in school is that he wants to work from a position of strength. School makes him stronger. Being a high school dropout with rich parents—that wouldn't be a very strong choice. And there are things he needs to learn. He respects education."

Thinking back to his first audition, Luke recalls, "The moment I picked up those sides that first day, I felt this part was mine! Oh, man, they got to take me! They got to, they got to!

"The scene I read was that monologue from the first episode where Dylan tried to call his parents in Paris. He talks French to the person who answers. Luckily I had learned a minimal amount of French. So I came in and delivered the monologue in French. I looked around the room when I finished and everyone's mouth was hanging open. 'It said to say it in French,' I said. 'Yeah, but no one else said it in French!'"

Sometimes Luke is as cool as Dylan, sometimes he isn't. "When I went to network for my reading, I puked. Me and James Eckhouse"—the actor who plays Mr. Walsh—"were together in this little room, kind of circling each other and breathing, trying to keep our nerves under control. It wasn't working for me, so I had to run to the bathroom and puke. I had to go back to network twice. I got so nervous. Even thinking back on it, I bite my nails.

"Dylan has a lot of worries. He chooses to take

on things in his life that a lot of young people don't. He's an alcoholic. He has an addictive personality. There's an inner strength in Dylan, set off by an equally strong vulnerability. A lot of things get to him."

Luke emphasizes that he is Luke and Dylan is Dylan. "Dylan is a lot different from me," he says. "I have to constantly keep in perspective the things that are him and the things that are me—the way he'd react in some circumstances versus the way I'd react. Now that I've been playing Dylan for a while, a lot of his character is ingrained in me. A lot has become second nature. Sometimes, though, I feel challenged, not knowing how he'd act in a certain situation. I find out as I do it. I'm not a method actor. I know what works for me."

The art of working successfully in a series is shading the character, episode by episode, so that by the end of a season, changes are evident. As Gabrielle Carteris observes, "When Luke started playing Dylan, the character was a James Dean type. Now it's a Luke Perry type."

Luke describes how he has followed this shading process with Dylan: "Dylan has progressed. The program has shown a lot of different sides of the character. I don't think he's progressed fast enough, but that's the nature of television. There have been some elements of the character we haven't been completely true to, but on the whole I've been very happy with what the writers have come up with.

"There have been a lot of changes in Dylan since the first episode. He's a lot more vulnerable now, not just toward Brenda, but toward the whole world. He's a little less shut off, a little more accessible now, and he's paying the price for it. In the beginning he came on as this slick dude with no problems he couldn't handle, just real cool. Now we've seen that he's not even close to perfect. He's got some real problems. That's real. No one is as bitchin' as he pretended to be.

"Look at the episode early this season where he slept alone in the beach club cabana. You see him there at his most vulnerable. He actually cries, remembering what his father once promised: 'I'll always be here for you.' Then the next morning Brandon shows up and Dylan immediately puts up his defenses again, acting like nothing ever really bothers him.

"Dylan's in a dangerous position. A lot of bad things could happen to someone with the opportunities and options he has. That's what it's all about—choices. We've got to hope Dylan doesn't make the wrong choices. You know what? I don't know which way he'll go.

"I liked that first episode when he sneaked his friends into the hotel where he lives, as if he were pulling off something big. He wants to create a little excitement in life, a little mystery. He's one part P. T. Barnum, one part something else.

"The producers and the writers give us more input than on many shows. I'll talk with Chuck Rosin about what I think should happen, and what he has in mind, and we'll come to some sort of compromise. I like that. I don't get carte blanche. The show is a collaborative effort all around. I'm just glad they listen to what I have to say.

"Dylan and Brandon have some funny moments. There's not a lot to laugh about in Dylan's world. At the same time, he's in the same world as the rest of us are. I can find humor everywhere. But I like keeping close to Dylan's darker edge. Besides, with Ian on the show we don't need any more comedy from the rest of us."

Bringing the part back home a little, Luke says, "Dylan is a product of the cinema and television. He's a video junkie. A lot of his character comes from Gary Cooper in *High Noon*. He's one part Starsky, one part Hutch. One part Larry, one part Moe"—from the *Three Stooges*. "A little bit of cynicism, a little bit of comedy."

What part did 'Starsky and Hutch" really play in Luke's upbringing? "'Starsky and Hutch' came on at a time in my life when I had no positive male role models. Maybe I saw in the show what I wanted to see. It certainly helped me through some hard times. That's when I made my big bond with television."

Luke swears he's no dime-store James Dean. "I chalk that comparison up to the misfortune of the draw. I happen to have a slight resemblance to him. You're born with whatever you look like. It's not fair to lay that on anybody. From Matt Dillon to Mickey Rourke, people always want to tag actors the new James Dean. The one name never changes, the other always does. There's always a new 'new James Dean.' James Dean is not in my game plan. I've been offered the role of Dean. I turned it down. It's a no-win situation. If you play it well, you're stuck. And where can you go after that, if it turns out you suck?"

The James Dean comparison is sure to dog Luke until he's forty. It is apt in a way, for Luke, like Dean, comes from the rural Midwest—Ohio in his case, Indiana in Dean's. Luke was born in Mansfield, Ohio, and he grew up in Fredericktown, a largely Amish farming community of 2,299 souls in the middle of the state. It's a place you either leave early or never escape. From an early age Luke knew he would be hitting the road one day, and he knew where he would be going: Hollywood.

"I've always been a big fan of television and movies," he says, describing the genesis of his desire to become an actor. "You go through stages of wanting to be a fireman or a policeman or go to sea. I just never left the stage of wanting to be an actor. The one thing I always came back to was that I wanted to be on TV, I wanted to be in the movies. I always felt a very strong connection to the people I saw on TV. I was the kind of person who sat there in Ohio and felt they were talking to me. I wanted to get inside there and be with them.

"I got kicked out of the school play when I was a sophomore for making obscene gestures. The play was *South Pacific,* and they wanted me to play one of the children of this dude. I was frustrated because I thought I was a better actor than the geek they chose to play the lead, and I didn't get it. That was my first lesson in professionalism: there are no small parts. But I didn't know that then, so I messed around.

"Fredericktown High School was a very over-bearing place. The school was so discipline-oriented, it forgot that there were other things that needed to be taught. It wasn't altogether a fun experience for me. They put me through a lot of shit.

"My discipline problem sprang from the fact that I question authority. But if authority is truly authoritative, and they really should be in power over others, then they don't mind being questioned. My teachers, however, didn't want to be questioned. Now I believe it's because half of them didn't know what they were doing. At a very young age I had an extensive vocabulary, and in a debate-type forum I could go head to head with any teacher in the school. My teachers wouldn't let me, because they knew they couldn't take me one-on-one, so they would always pull rank and send me to the office.

"They called it disruption. I called it seeking clarification. I think people should respect their elders, but only if the elders prove to be respectable. You should respect someone just because they have a few years on you? They gotta have more on the ball than that."

Grades? "I wasn't scholastically dazzling, you know. For me, school was a series of captive audiences. I was real good at 'Jeopardy,' so there you go. I love that show. It's the greatest game show of all time on TV. I did test once to get on it, but I did not qualify. It was a tough test.

"Fredericktown is a small town. There were just eighty-seven people in my graduating class. I remember graduation. This is the type of school it was. They told us that at graduation anyone who threw his hat in the air at the end wouldn't receive a diploma. I said, 'You gotta be kidding me!' The end of the ceremony came, and everyone looked at me and said, 'Luke, whadda we do?' I said, 'When I say three, we throw these hats.' The teachers should have known better.

"Once they put two of my friends on in-school suspension. So me and a couple of my buddies dressed up like bandits and went in there with fake guns and broke them out. It was quite something. We about gave that old school secretary a heart attack, kicking the office door open and yelling, 'Nobody fucking move! Nobody!' They all just froze. It was great!

"Of course, I was later disciplined by the principal, but he said, 'I gotta tell you, that was really funny.' Actually Phil, the principal, he was a good guy. A lot of times he would tell me flat out, 'It's my job. I've got to do this. There's nothing particularly wrong with what you're doing, but everyone has to answer to somebody.'"

All in all, Luke prefers adulthood to being a kid. "There's one thing about being an adult, and it's the thing I like best: you only have to answer to the law and the man who signs your paycheck. That's it. Everything comes down to personal choice. I've always been willing to take responsibility for my actions. That goes along with adulthood. It's not as if you're eighteen and suddenly there are no rules. You have to take responsibility.

"My parents got a little sick of having me get

called into the principal's office all the time. But I never hurt anyone. I wasn't violent. I was bored, and I wanted to amuse myself. So I did. If I amused a few others along the way, there's no harm done.

"I wasn't what you'd call a class clown. What I did was more of an art form. A class clown is the kid who sits in the back and makes faces and gets the bright idea to throw a spitball. I was more like stand-up comedy waiting to happen. My routine was to play the devil's advocate. The teacher would lay down some law and say this is how it must be, and I'd automatically ask, 'What if it was like this or like that, instead?'

"I always loved sports, though I did have a problem with organized rules. I ran track and played tennis and some baseball. I was too small for football. By the time I graduated I was one of the better basketball players in the school, although I never went out for the team. We always played together over at the park."

Luke's school discipline problems helped ensure that he wouldn't go on to college. "I never wanted to go, because I knew that what I needed to know to be an actor I wouldn't learn at college. I would like to study criminology. That's fascinating. At one time I thought about being a lawyer. Then I thought, eight more years of school? Noooooo!

"My teachers used to come down on me my junior and senior year for not preparing for college, and I'd say, 'Look. I'm going to be an actor. I know what I need to know. You're not teaching it. I'm not paying attention.' That was my constant refrain. I told so many people, I finally figured I'd better get my ass on out there and do it. I had to walk it like I'd talked it.

"I'd been planning to get out of town and come to Hollywood as long as I could remember. I couldn't do it till I got out of high school. It's your own life then. One day a couple of months after graduation I just said, 'Well, Mom, I'm leaving,' and I jammed on out here." It was the summer of 1985.

"Me and another guy, Michael, we drove on out in this tiny car, a Sunbird. He had lived in California before and he wanted to come back. He had some friends, and we slept on their couch and floor for a while. Then we got jobs and moved into motels. I lived in motels in Orange County for a year and a half, different ones all the time.

"That wasn't the highlight of my personal career. I did learn a lot of things. Oh, man, I worked on the assembly line in a doorknob factory. I did demonstrations in supermarkets. It was heinous. I did telephone sales. I laid a lot of asphalt. Shoveled a lot, painted a lot. I painted lines in parking lots, including the lines in the lot here at Torrance High School. That is hilarious."

Luke was in California, but he wasn't acting. He could see the Hollywood sign, but he wasn't in Hollywood. He could watch TV, but he was just as far away from being on TV as he had been in Ohio. Orange County is best known as the home of Disneyland, but there aren't many actors there, except the ones playing Mickey Mouse and Snow White at the park.

"Come on, who are we kidding?" Luke says, explaining his delay in seeking to realize his acting dreams. "You don't go direct from the farm to Hollywood. You just don't do it. First I had to acclimate myself, find out what southern California was all about, and see if I could stomach living out here. Then it would be time to go and get into the little world of Hollywood.

"I finally saved up some money and moved out of Orange County and up to Hollywood. I said bye-bye to my friends—'I got to do it, and I got to do it now!'—and I moved up to Hollywood by myself."

Hollywood is a district of Los Angeles where the film industry started. Just one major studio—Paramount—remains. But the area retains hundreds of small businesses that serve the film and TV industries, and residential rents are low enough to attract thousands upon thousands of young men and women who aim to become actors.

"For as many people as there are, there are that many different ways to become an actor," Luke says, speaking at last from the point of view of an actor who has succeeded. "No two people need choose the same way. So I find it very difficult to give advice, because it never really applies. It all depends on the person. You have to learn as you go."

Of his own experience, Luke remembers, "I started going to acting class. Someone introduced me to an agent. I started going on auditions. A year and a half, two years later, I got something." In the meantime, Luke kept his head above water doing the short-term, odd-hours, no-future jobs that actors customarily take. Before that final gig as a construction company estimator, he cashed some pretty miscellaneous checks: "I cooked breakfast at a tennis club. I did a little chauffeuring. Actors are notorious for being waiters.

"A casting director named Bobby Hoffman was the first to take an interest in me and tell me I would work. I went up for a show he was casting, and he told me, 'You're not going to get this part. You're not physically right. But you're really good. Keep coming back, because you will get a part.' Sure enough, next time in, he got me the job.

"What held me up for a long time was that I didn't belong to the Screen Actors Guild. In order to be an actor you have to be in SAG, but in order to be in SAG you have to be an actor. It's Catch-22. I couldn't beat it for a long time. Finally I did.

"I became more focused on what I was doing. I raised my performance level. I worked with better actors, better than me. I learned from them. Once I saw how serious everyone else was about it, I realized, man, if I don't get serious they're gonna eat me up. They'll blow me away.

"I became fascinated with the craft of acting. It's very cerebral, you know. If it looks effortless, like I'm just standing there and doing it, that means I'm doing it right. You can't look self-conscious. You have to be natural, and that's the hard part.

"I got my first job from Hoffman, on a daytime series, 'Loving.' I read for the part in his office. He put my reading on tape and sent the tape to ABC in New York. New York said, 'Screen-test Luke.' They screen-tested me and then New York said, 'Fly Luke in.' They put me up in a hotel in New York. I met the girl who played the part opposite my character, and I taped a scene with her on the actual set of the show. I did that. Then I flew back to L.A. The next day they called me and said, 'Pack up, come back to New York. You've got the job.'

"ABC had tested me for a lot of jobs before, and they had never hired me. 'Loving' was on-the-job training. Trial by fire. I played a country boy from Tennessee named Ned Bates. Ned was nice to the point of being stupid. He was the kind of guy whose girlfriend was a prostitute, selling herself to other men, but she wouldn't sleep with Ned. A lot of things like that happened to Ned. I did the part for a year, and then in one episode I went upstairs to wash my hands and was never seen again! As far as the audience is concerned I'm still up there, getting cleaner and cleaner." Maybe Ned went to Europe, like everybody else who leaves a soap without dying or going into a coma.

"I stayed in New York and did a couple of Levi's commercials. I was on another show, 'Another World,' on and off for about six months. I don't even remember my character. His name was Kenny, I recall that much. I was in a movie called *Terminal Bliss*. I did a small part in another movie, called *Scorchers*, with Faye Dunaway and James Earl Jones, which will finally be coming out this Christmas. Watch closely, because if you blink, you'll miss me. I played Ray Ray LaPugh, a Cajun, a crazy, dirty, filthy, stinking-drunk trapper. Loved it! I got to grow a beard for the part. Cool!

"After that I wasn't getting any more work in New York, so I came back out here about two months before this show happened. I figured my chances were better. Turned out they were."

Yes, indeed. Luke has found his stride on "Beverly Hills, 90210. "I really enjoy working on the show," he says. "It's a job that promotes peace of mind. I have something to concentrate on full-time. I need that. I'm not usually a very focused person until I get into something deeply. Once I do, I want to make sure I get all I can out of it before I move on.

"These guys I'm working with here, aside from being really outstanding actors, are fun to be around. When the show first started to become successful and the audience numbers grew and grew, we looked at each other, like, wow! Can you believe it? That lasted about one minute. Immediately afterward we put our heads down and got back to work. Now we work together to keep everything in check. We're real serious about what we're doing. We realize that if we don't deliver, we're history. This group is more together than any group of actors I've ever been involved with. When you spend this much time with people, you either love them or hate them. Luckily, most of us *love* each other.

"I've spent time off the set with everybody in the cast. I just love 'em all. Mostly the girls do the girl things. We're good at the guy things. They're good at shopping.

"I hang out a lot with Jason and Ian. There's no pretending between us. We've been through some tough spots together. That builds friendship. Ian and I knew each other in New York. We were already buddies there. Eye and I was buds. We were both on soaps at the same time and met each other at various soap events. We played softball together.

"Now we've become very good friends. Out here the three of us are separated from our families—Vancouver, New Jersey, Ohio—so we're family for each other, and give support. They're great guys, not to mention the others in the cast. If I didn't feel that way about them, I'd punch out at the end of the day and I'd go my separate way. But all of us will come in on our days off just to see each other and see what's going on.

"Jason and Eye and I do your typical guy things. We get together and watch a game on TV. We go out, you know . . . meet women. We shoot pool, have a coupla beers. We went skeet shooting. We do things guys do, not big TV-star stuff. I feel better going out with them than by myself. If we get recognized, there's strength in numbers."

Luke handles the sudden onslaught of fans' interest in him by holding his breath and letting it wash right over him. Early experiences with the energizing effect of personal appearances were followed by a resolution not to become addicted to adulation. His attitude now is that "I do not allow myself to think about that aspect. You can't let the fans get to you, otherwise you'd shut yourself in your house and become a recluse. I don't allow myself to think about the fame thing, so stop bringing it up! That's not my job, being famous. My job is to act."

Jennie Garth is the opposite of Kelly Taylor. Kelly is an incredibly rich bitch, and Jennie is sweet and unsophisticated. "Innocent" is a better word. But because of who Jennie is, we've been able to add layers of complexity to Kelly. She'll always be concerned about social status, but now you can see why she's like that, and you'll see she's capable of being a caring person. Jennie is able to convey both the facade outside and the reality inside.

—DARREN STAR

Jennie grew up on a farm a long way from Beverly Hills, yet she's so good at playing sophisticated Kelly. That's acting! I've watched her for over a year, and there's never been one false moment, not one. She's been able to take the character from being a totally closed Beverly Hills princess to someone capable of a full range of emotions.

—CHUCK ROSIN

First we were intrigued by Jennie's looks. She's just so beautiful! Because Brenda is dark, Kelly should be a blonde. She had to have the self-assurance of wealth—without making you dislike her for it. Jennie could do that, so we chose her, still wondering if she could handle real drama. We finally gave her a chance in the episode about her mother's drug and booze problem, and she knocked us out. Jennie showed that Miss Know-It-All Kelly had a lot more to her than snobbishness.

—AARON SPELLING

Jennie Garth

WHEN KELLY TAYLOR FIRST APPEARED ON screen in "Beverly Hills, 90210," viewers braced themselves for a thoroughly unsympathetic character. She wore the clothes of a villainess, and she had the position and manner of a character who could only mean trouble for naive newcomer Brenda Walsh.

But the producers of the show were more clever than that. When casting the show, they foresaw that even the queen of West Beverly could turn out to have a heart. They chose an actress who could simulate the pettiness of a high school snob while crying out between the lines, "I'm actually nice!"

Jennie Garth is the unanimous choice for Sweetest "Beverly Hills, 90210" Cast Member. Jennie comes from rural Illinois, far from Rodeo Drive. She's more accustomed to riding horses than BMWs. Jennie was shoveling manure when Kelly was buying her first pearl necklace. She was doing 4-H projects in the midst of a large and loving family when Kelly was putting her drunken mother to bed. Jennie did not grow up too soon, and she remains unspoiled.

Here's her account of how the part came to her, after a long, bumpy journey: "It was pilot season of 1990, and quite a few teen-oriented shows were casting. I read for 'Hull High' and was offered a part. Then at the tail end of pilot season I heard rumors about Aaron Spelling's high school show, which was going to be casting soon. I told my managers I wanted a chance at 'Class of Beverly Hills,' which was the title then, and I said I'd be selling myself short if I took 'Hull High.' So I passed on 'Hull High,' which was the scariest thing I'd ever done, because I'd never had an offer like that before. At that time, I hadn't even seen the 'Beverly Hills' script.

"I read for 'Beverly Hills,' and it didn't look like I'd get it. Some of the people who were deciding on casting thought I definitely wasn't right. A few others were pulling for me. I set my mind to it. It dragged on for weeks. I went back five or six times, and in between I kept studying the script. To tell the truth, I thought the script was a little flat and one-dimensional, because it devoted so little time to establishing all the characters. But I anticipated that there would be great opportunities for the characters to evolve and add layers later, and that's exactly what has happened since then.

"While I was waiting for the callbacks, I kept going to my acting classes and working on the script with my acting coach every night. I kept getting these conflicting messages back from the 'Beverly Hills, 90210' production company and the network. I would hear that so-and-so liked me for the part and so-and-so-someone-else didn't think I was right. I guess there was a battle between those who thought I could bring a lot to Kelly and those who didn't like me. I knew I was right for the part. I knew I wouldn't get it.

"The time I went to read in Mr. Spelling's office, with all these people staring at me, twenty people in this huge room—that was the most nerve-racking. I was so nervous waiting! Food and cigarettes and stuff were all set out at our disposal, as if we'd be waiting a long time. My manager kept licking his fingers and patting my hair down, trying to calm me down and failing badly. When I finally went in to Mr. Spelling's office, it was extra-intimidating because of all the pictures of all the stars of Mr. Spelling's shows, like 'Charlie's Angels' and 'Dynasty.' Such a legacy! But Mr. Spelling was so gracious. He got up and hugged me, because he knows how frightened people can be when they go in there. Everybody looked me up and down, and then I did the scene. I guess I was okay because here I am!

"Previously I'd done some characters that were over-the-top, obnoxiously mean, and I guess that's why I was considered for Kelly. I'm really unlike her. I come from a very close-knit family. I grew up on a farm in a small town in the Midwest. I never even met anyone like Kelly when I was growing up. She never even crossed my mind, because nobody like her ever lived near me. But I'm a people-watcher. My father and I used to go and sit in the mall and just watch people. I can pick up characteristics of people, and somehow they organize themselves in my mind, and that's how I create a character.

"Kelly is so far off from me. She's a challenge. There are no limitations. As Kelly, I can be as mean or as wild as I want. That's so much fun! If I played a character who was similar to me, I'd go to work and be bored every day. Playing Kelly, I can be wacky and loony."

Every large-cast drama benefits from a bitch. "Dallas" and "Dynasty" had to have someone who was richer and meaner than everyone else. "On the surface, Kelly looks like that type of person," Jennie agrees. "The Joan Collins who is the lady everyone loves to despise. Or Donna Mills.

"But there are sympathetic sides to Kelly. We've explored her family life, and now that people know that background, she's not so hate-able. Her background justifies the unkind things she does—no, not justifies them, lets you see where they come from. She grew up on her own, we now know. Her mother was an alcoholic. Kelly had to do everything on her own. At sixteen she has to have all the knowledge, all the wisdom, of an adult. There's a lot of pressure on her, and all in all she's handled it well. She's a leader. When it comes down to it, she takes care of her friends.

"We all have to wait around for our episode, the

one that gives our character another dimension. At the beginning maybe Kelly was over the top. We needed to establish who she was and that she was the bitch, the snob of the school. She had all the money and all the men and she could have anything she wanted. Then we see her go home and find out what it's like to see her mother passed out on the bed or doing cocaine or drinking. I finally confront my mother and say, 'I can't grow up alone. I need you. You haven't been there for me. I need you now.' And then I have to go back to school the next day and pretend that nothing is happening. It's amazing that she can do that—but that must be why she acts mean sometimes.

"There was another episode that showed how growing up so fast can be harmful. When Kelly loses her virginity, it happens too fast, not the way she wanted it. It's not a good experience for her—though you wouldn't think that just to look at her or hear her sometimes.

"Now Kelly's mother has been to rehab and she's sober, and they've become like a mother-daughter friend type of team."

Some dramas can lose their edge when the unsympathetic characters become too nice, and Jennie is aware of that danger. "Yes, there's a fine line with Kelly. The show's writers and I have got to keep Kelly on the edge, where you love her and you hate her, too. The most fun is when you hate her, when you say, 'I can't believe Kelly did that!' And I think that people see Kelly and ask themselves, 'I wonder if I've ever been mean like that.' I also like to show that Kelly can be a good friend. I get lots of letters from viewers who write me with their problems because they see something sympathetic and helpful in Kelly—and then they tell me their problems, thinking I'll be sympathetic and helpful!"

A good example of an episode that showed both sides of Kelly at the same time came early in the second season of 'Beverly Hills, 90210.' Kelly flirted with one of the beach club's volleyball kings until he finally asked her out. But when she tried to accelerate their relationship by jumping naked into the surf, he didn't respond. Only after lots of moaning and recriminations did Kelly accept the fact that a boy could like her without being sexually attracted to her.

Jennie says, "That episode danced around the subject of whether the boy might be gay. He had confusing thoughts, anyway. It devastated Kelly that someone would turn her down. She'd never experienced that before. At first she didn't know how to handle it. She was hurt. She felt ugly. So she just left. She didn't want to deal with those feelings. Yet she knew he was a nice guy who was confused and reaching out for help. When she saw Steve picking on him, she stuck up for him. She showed her compassionate side and became a good friend. She came through for him. That's realistic, because once you get to know someone, nothing else matters except if they're a good person."

The writers on the show regularly consult with the actors, Jennie reports. "They ask me if I'm comfortable with their ideas. Can I justify Kelly doing such and such? One story line they checked out with me was when David Silver's father started dating my mother. Kelly had to be gracious to the biggest geek in the school! She has a hard time with that, so the story line is very funny. David is ecstatic, of course, to get close to a campus queen like Kelly. Then Kelly pulls a little stunt. She's really rude to David and his father. The father says, 'What is so great about this girl? She's mean and she's cruel and she doesn't have any heart.' She seems like she really is heartless, too. Eventually she and David find they can understand each other."

What Kelly does for the girls of "Beverly Hills, 90210," Steve does for the boys. "Kelly and Steve are kind of the same character," Jennie theorizes, "but different sexes. They're both from the same background. They're both rich and popular. As the show has progressed, Steve hasn't opened up as much. In the story lines we've been given, they've tried to make Kelly more compassionate and sympathetic and relatable and keep Steve crazy and wild and a bad influence on everybody. At the same time, Steve is obviously a guy who thinks about things—but that doesn't mean he'll stop doing them!

"Steve and Kelly used to go out. They were together for a couple of years and fought constantly. They still fight constantly, to this day. They're so much alike, they can't possibly be together. They have to be just friends.

"Kelly has a quick wit. She can mix it with the best of them. She doesn't take stuff from anyone. She can be very sarcastic. She says what she feels, and sometimes what she feels is pretty silly. She can laugh at herself. Donna, on the other hand, is ding-y through and through. Kelly likes Donna because she likes being looked up to and she likes the idea of teaching Donna the ropes. Plus, they grew up together and they both drive BMWs—you know how that goes.

"Kelly has a different relationship with Brenda. She instantly felt a friendship as soon as Brenda moved in. Kelly doesn't know why, because Brenda couldn't be more opposite from her. Somehow she felt like a sister to Brenda. She can help Brenda fit in at West Beverly and be the leader. Also, Kelly definitely likes hanging out with the Walshes, who are real parents. She likes feeling part of that family and getting advice on how to deal with her mother.

"Kelly was attracted to Brandon at first—who wouldn't be! There was this challenge to get him to like her. She's successful in getting him to kiss her. But for him it's like kissing his sister. She understands, and he becomes a brother figure for her. They're pals, even if they don't hang out together.

"Dylan? She's attracted to him—she's not stupid. She doesn't understand him. She's never been around so deep a person or someone with such problems and experiences. He's so cute, but I don't know if she'll ever get the chance to know him better. Dylan might never see that she'd like to learn from him—or the show's writers won't! He is Brenda's boyfriend, after all, and Kelly has to respect that.

"It was interesting when we had the camping episode and we were all together in a small space. All

Jason Priestley as Brandon Walsh.

Jason Priestley and Shannen Doherty as Brandon and Brenda Walsh.

Television's favorite family, the Walshes. *Clockwise:* James Eckhouse as Jim Walsh, Carol Potter as Cindy Walsh, Jason Priestley as Brandon Walsh, and Shannen Doherty as Brenda Walsh.

Luke Perry as Dylan McKay.

The Beverly Hills Beauties. *Left to right* - Jennie Garth as Kelly Taylor, Shannen Doherty as Brenda Walsh, and Tori Spelling as Donna Martin.

Behind the scenes on Beverly Hills, 90210. *Left to right:* Ian Ziering as Steve Sanders, Luke Perry as Dylan McKay, and Jason Priestley as Brandon Walsh.

Television's most wanted men. Jason Priestley as
Brandon Walsh and Luke Perry as Dylan McKay.

Gabrielle Carteris as
Andrea Zuckerman.

Brian Austin
Green as
David Silver.

Shannen Doherty as Brenda Walsh.

Jennie Garth as Kelly Taylor.

Tori Spelling as Donna Martin.

Just hanging out. *Clockwise:* Jason Priestley, Ian Ziering, and Luke Perry.

On the set with Shannen Doherty and Jennie Garth.

Checking out the scene at West Beverly High. Ian Ziering as Steve Sanders and Luke Perry as Dylan McKay.

Vamping it up as the hottest new singing group. *Left to right:* Jennie Garth, Shannen Doherty, and Tori Spelling.

Hear no evil, see no evil, speak no evil. *Left to right:* Ian Ziering, Luke Perry, and Jason Priestley.

The beauty on the beach. Top: Tori Spelling. *Bottom left to right:* Jason Priestley, Luke Perry, Ian Ziering, and Brian Austin Green.

Luke Perry as mysterious, cool character, Dylan McKay.

First love. Luke Perry and Shannen Doherty as Dylan McKay and Brenda Walsh.

Jason Priestley and Gabrielle Carteris as Brandon Walsh and Andrea Zuckerman.

Jason Priestley and Luke Perry as Brandon Walsh and Dylan McKay.

The cast of Beverly Hills, 90210. *Clockwise from the top:*
Gabrielle Carteris, Jason Priestley, Tori Spelling, Brian Austin
Green, Jennie Garth, Ian Ziering, Luke Perry, and Shannen
Doherty.

the characters got along! Sitting around the fire, discussing the meaning of life. It turned out that Kelly and Andrea, of all people, had some of the same thoughts. Kelly felt that the meaning of life is love, and Andrea said the same thing, elaborating on the idea."

Jennie has happily joined in the one-for-all, all-for-one spirit on the set of "Beverly Hills, 90210." She says, "The cast has got to be a tight-knit unit. For one thing, all our dressing rooms are next to each other on the same hall, and everybody can hear everything everyone else is saying. We've developed quite a healthy camaraderie. We have to be close, whether we like it or not! There are no secrets. We respect each other's space. We all get along, and that's why it's a joy to come to work.

"I guess I hang out most with Gabrielle. We're both the homemaking type—we like cooking and cleaning. We go to exercise class together sometimes. Shannen—I've gone dancing with her. It's amazing we'd want to spend time with each other after a fourteen-hour workday, but we do—sometimes, at least. I must say that the boys go off and do their own thing most of the time. They're all wild and crazy, and when they go out, I'd rather go home and sleep!

"We like getting together as a group. Sometimes we watch the show and have dinner together. We did that for the premiere of the second year. We all went to Darren Star's house"—Darren is the creator of the show—"and watched it and laughed at each other or said that something else that somebody did was great. We critiqued the show until there was nothing left of it!

"I can take just about anything any of the others throw at me. I'm my own worst critic. Anyway, you know when they're joking. They're not really ragging on you. If they had something to say, they'd take you aside and whisper, 'Jen, that was . . . *Awful!*' But nobody's done that yet. We get a lot of that brother-sister stuff, joking around. The boys beat on each other and wrestle constantly, just to burn off energy. We all fight and chase each other, like in a family.

"We're all young—that sums it up. We like to have a good time. The other night, my boyfriend's band was playing at a club, and Shannen came with her boyfriend and hung out and watched. That was nice, even though I'm not a club person. I like staying home or going to the movies. Shannen likes going out more. Gabrielle—she loves going dancing. Jason will go out with you, but he won't dance.

"I've had crazy, crazy, crazy times with Ian. We used to go out, with my boyfriend at the time and his girlfriend at the time. We've both 'evolved' since then. Ian took me skiing with a group of friends, and we had a blast. I wasn't a very good skier, but Ian was Mr. Ski Man, right? He was playing Mr. Macho. We went up the lift, and I didn't know how to get off the lift. We're at the top of this really steep mountain. 'Here, let me help you,' Ian said, but instead of sliding off the seat and skiing away, I just held on. Our poles got tangled, and we fell together. He was up instantly, looking around to see if anyone noticed that he'd fallen. It was the funniest thing! I just lay there and laughed. It was the first time he'd fallen in five years, he claimed. I think Ian is the funniest man alive, the funniest person in the world."

Sometimes the constant horsing around on the set gets to be too much, Jennie says. "One time we were all in this little room preparing to do a scene, and we were so close together and tense. The assistant director kept shouting, 'Will everybody please be quiet! Let's try to get this done!'

"Jason and Luke were behind the camera. I was nearby, minding my own business, listening to the director. They were horsing around like boys do, and fighting to get rid of the tension. Jason took a fake swing at Luke, aiming to miss, of course. Luke dodged unexpectedly. Jason's fist bopped me square on the nose! I was on my back for twenty minutes, like in shock! Unable to function, gushing tears. Jason felt sooooo bad!

"Whenever it's a joke and something unexpected happens on the set, it always happens to me. I'm always the one who gets hit in the head—it's like it's in some script! Once we were shooting outdoors and for some reason the crew was throwing this rope up into a tree and over a branch. Of course, as soon as Luke and Jason saw that, they were both going, 'Hey, let me! I can do it!' So I'm sitting nowhere near this, in the middle of a bunch of people, and I'm the one that gets hit on the head with this thick, heavy noose!

"Here's another time: Just yesterday a prop girl was putting a watch on somebody else's wrist. I'm just standing there minding my own business, nothing to do with the watch or the prop girl. Somehow the prop girl's elbow comes flying out and pokes me in the temple! I just always get beat on. I can't cry anymore. I just laugh! What's going to happen next?

"I'm always in the wrong place at the wrong time. Never before this show. 'Beverly Hills, 90210' is a jinx—I just figured it out! But nobody believes it. One episode, I had to do a scene where I'm driving and talking on my car phone. That's so L.A.! I'm doing this complicated maneuver in the middle of rush hour traffic on San Vicente Boulevard, one of the main drags in town. I did the scene once, and then they told me to drive back, make an illegal U-turn and go down a mile and do another U-turn, and drive back here again. This was pretty nerve-racking. I was left out there in traffic like a little lost sheep. But I was lucky—no accident."

Jennie finds people-watching hard to do now, since so many people recognize her. "I feel if I make eye contact with anybody, they'll recognize me, so I usually walk along with my eyes down. I do get recognized sometimes, usually when I'm about to take a big old bite of spaghetti.

"When I was younger I never wrote fan letters to anyone on TV. I never felt anyone on TV was any kind of role model. But I guess other people are different. I still wonder why anybody would think I'm so great that they need to have a piece of paper with my name on it.

"The mail I get is interesting. There's one girl who writes me, I swear, three times a week—typed—and draws pictures. Her name is Tammy. I haven't written her back yet. Maybe I'll get around to that."

Instead of watching television and writing fan letters, Jennie grew up staying busy on her parents' horse farm in Champaign, Illinois. Champaign-Urbana is the site of the University of Illinois, so life in Jennie's hometown wasn't all sucking hayseeds.

"I have four sisters and two brothers," she says. "I grew up in a house with three of my sisters—the others are older and had moved out. They all had their chores. My sister Cammy and I are the girly-girls, and we liked to stay indoors. My other two sisters are tomboy types who were up at the crack of dawn doing the horses thing. My father is such a character. He liked to bring home animals. He'd bring home a chicken, and that would be our project, and before we knew it, there would be nineteen million chickens running around. He'd go through that phase, and then he'd bring home a pig and pretty soon there would be nineteen million piglets.

"It was a horse farm. We didn't raise corn or anything like that. My father was a horse trainer. I had the best childhood ever imaginable. It's almost sad to look back on it, because I keep wishing it was still the same, but it never will be again. My family home was built by my father and my brothers from the ground up. I watched it rise."

As the youngest girl, Jennie had fewer chores to perform than the rest of the family. "Sometimes they forced me to clean out the horse stalls, but it wasn't my regular job. I had a horse of my own, and I did take care of him. I showed him in competitions, and he won a lot, because he was such a great horse. He was my best friend. I was involved in 4-H and all the silly things we do in the Midwest. My 4-H projects were horses, always horses.

"One time they were giving out a 'clean pen' award at the county fair. This is really silly! I *vacuumed* my horse's *stall*! I just wanted that award so bad, they had to give it to me. I was set to get that award! It would have crushed me for life if I hadn't won."

Keen horsewoman though she was, Jennie had artistic interests, too. "My mom put me in dance class. Some kids like to do it. Others just do it because their moms like to watch them doing it. I loved it. I was in shows in high school and different places around Phoenix. I got to be pretty good, but I knew I wasn't cut out for a career as a dancer. I didn't have the discipline or the body. I couldn't hack being part of a company. I wasn't very little or very thin. I was content to teach.

"I remember teaching these five-year-olds to tap-dance. They were so cute. They never actually got it, but everyone had a lot of fun. Ballet was my specialty, and I taught ballet, too. I was managing the studio and working with the owner. I hated to do it, but when I left for Los Angeles I stopped dancing. I couldn't spread myself so thin."

When Jennie was thirteen, the Garths moved to Phoenix because her father had a heart condition. Jennie remembers, "He kept having heart attacks. He had bypass operations, and then he needed to get out of the humid weather in Illinois. I'm very close to my father. I'd get up in the morning, and he'd make me breakfast, and we'd go out and sit in the woods, watching things. He taught me a lot about everything. My dad's the greatest. It was traumatic to see him lying helpless in the hospital. He's better now, and he's back to being the crazy guy he always was.

"When we moved to Arizona, we took my horse, my sister's horse, and one of my dad's. We were like a Gypsy convoy traveling across the country, the Garth clan in our four cars and horse trucks and moving vans. We bought a home with stables, but my sisters grew up and it got to the point where we had to sell the horses. We slowly got out of the horse business. Nobody wanted to sell that last horse, but we did, and we moved to the city and I went to this big school with lots of kids.

"You can adapt to anything at that age, if you're open to it. It was a choice my family made, and I dealt with it. My family always came first. I never rebelled, but I became more independent. I had a great life in Arizona, just as I had in Illinois. It was weirder for my mom and dad."

So Jennie was a normal corn-fed midwestern girl even in Arizona, until the day she entered a scholarship pageant. She was fifteen, and was good-looking enough to reach the state finals. "My friends from dance class conned me into doing it," she remembers. "I'd always been interested in dance, so it wasn't like I had no interest in being up on a stage.

"The contestants in the pageant had to stand around a lot with a number on our belts. I kept looking around in embarrassment wondering why my mother ever let me do it. It was one of those growing-up things. It was such a girly thing, with such a pretty dress. I'd never let a daughter of mine do it. I think she was happy I did it, going around saying, 'That's my daughter!'

"One of the judges at the contest was Randy James, a talent manager for a Los Angeles company. For some reason, in the speech all of us had to give, I said something about how it might be nice if I became an actress. When I got up to speak, I forgot my whole speech. Nerves took over, and I ad-libbed. I'd never done any acting, and I had no idea why I said I wanted to be an actress. 'Sounds good, I think I'll say it!'

"After the contest, Mr. James and his wife approached my mother and me. He said he'd be interested in seeing if I had any acting talent and possibly representing me. Sure, right, I thought. That's the last we'll hear from you. I didn't want to listen to anything he was saying. I wasn't interested in being an actress or even in being in this pageant. I came in third or something.

"A month later Mr. James called my mom and they rapped on the phone. Somehow it happened—I don't even remember how." Jennie started taking acting classes and began sending videotapes of her work to Randy James every week.

"My mom and I had a heart-to-heart talk about giving acting a shot. She said she'd be there for me the whole way. After that, we sold our house, and she quit her job, and I left school early. We just picked up and left. We came to Los Angeles and knocked on this guy's door and said, 'Hi! We're here!" He was a little nervous, to say the least.

"My mother and I got an apartment, a two-bedroom apartment, which we shared with three other people. My dad was still back in Arizona. We struggled here for a while. I started going to acting classes immediately. Everything happened in the blink of an eye. For four months I lived and breathed auditions and studying acting all day long.

"Suddenly I got a job—and it was the lead in a series! It was 'Brand New Town,' and I was playing the daughter of Barbara Eden—'I Dream of Jeannie' Eden, *that* Barbara Eden. I was ecstatic! The show went for about seven episodes before NBC canceled it. Okay, I said, that's what's supposed to happen out here, I'm supposed to struggle some more. So I went out and auditioned some more. I learned to fly on a trapeze for 'Circus of the Stars.' I did a 'Growing Pains' episode and some little Disney things"— "Teen Angel Returns," starring none other than Jason Priestley, and "Just Perfect." "I was just waiting for another project. Then 'Beverly Hills, 90210' happened.

"I'd never thought about acting. I thought I'd go to college, get an education degree, and open my own dance studio and teach dancing. But my life took a different turn and here I am.

"These days, my mother will go to a grocery store, and she'll pick up *TV Guide* while she's waiting in the checkout line. She'll open it to Thursday night, and there'll be this advertisement with a picture of me, right? She'll make sure some other woman is looking over her shoulder and then she'll go, 'That's my daughter!' My mom is so funny! My dad does it, too, though he can never say the full title of the show because he can't remember the zip code for Beverly Hills."

Jennie's mother is back in Arizona with Mr. Garth now because, as Jennie says, "It's time for Jennie to be on her own. My mother is doing the wife thing again. I invested my money from the show in buying a house. She comes back to L.A. every other week or so to help me out. We're adding on to the house I bought"—in Sherman Oaks not far from the "Beverly Hills, 90210" studio. "There's mass confusion, and she loves that. And my dog has been having puppies and wrecking my house, so it's nice to have my mother to share that with!"

"I bought the house in Arizona that my parents live in now. They make the payments, but it's in my name. All this real estate stuff comes about because another job my parents did when I was growing up was that they were Realtors. I worked in a realty office, so I know a bit about property myself. I decided I'd like to be a real estate mogul. That's what Ian calls me, 'the Mogul.' I'd like decorating and designing, anyway."

Ian is just as fun-loving as Steve Sanders, but he's a hundred percent less pretentious. He can play someone who's obnoxious and egocentric without being that way in reality at all. Like all the guys in the show, Ian is taking his success really well. There's a strong camaraderie among the guys and none of this "Ho-hum, another hit show."

—DARREN STAR

Ian is great at playing the buffoonishness of a Beverly Hills socialite. "This is my turf, my mom's a big star, I know everything that's going down." That's Steve. Ian doesn't have any of that high-and-mighty manner. He does have Steve's energy. There's a lot of Steve in Ian and a lot of Ian in Steve—though there's nothing offensive in Ian. Ian loves life. He attacks the hell out of it.

—AARON SPELLING

Ian brings boundless enthusiasm to his work. At first, Steve was just a preppy bad guy leading Brandon into temptation. We began to see Ian playing something else between the lines. There was a lot of hurt in Steve that Ian was conveying silently. Instead of a stereotype, Ian played a real human being with humor and humanity. That's paying off this year, now that we're not so busy establishing the Walsh household and the show is more an ensemble.

—CHUCK ROSIN

Ian Ziering

IF YOU'RE LOOKING FOR A LAUGH, STICK with Ian Ziering. His vigor keeps the "Beverly Hills, 90210" cast and crew alert and smiling even when the workday reaches the pumpkin hour. All of his co-workers come out spontaneously with comments like Shannen Doherty's: "Ian is an original. Ian Ziering is the funniest man alive!"

It isn't that Ian talks a lot. That's Jason's job. What Ian does is smile incessantly, as if he's just thought of the biggest joke in the world and he's about to let everybody else in on it. There's isn't an ounce of shyness in Ian. He is up front all the time.

"Everyone says he's the funniest member of the cast," Gabrielle Carteris says. "He always makes everybody feel great. At the same time, he's one of the most level-headed of the cast members. He's done a lot with his character, to make people not dislike him."

What we see on the show is only a small part of what Ian can do. Sure, Steve Sanders is a fun-loving guy, and people stay his friends because he does like to keep things light. David Silver points his camcorder at Steve and asks his opinion of life, and Steve responds, deadpan, "It's great to be young. I wish they all could be California girls. You know what I'm saying?" Steve is cool and funny, but his troublemaking side is predominant. In real life, though, Ian uses his cool and his heat to pump others up positively.

Ian had a hard time getting the part. Yet he tells his audition horror story as if it were a rollicking comedy. He's taking a break between scenes on the soundstage ten miles north of Beverly Hills where "Beverly Hills, 90210" shoots its interiors. He whips off his shirt—here's a great chance to work on his tan!—and leads the way outside, where he sits cross-legged in the middle of the sidewalk and says, "Let's talk!"

He begins, "It was called 'Class of Beverly Hills' when I auditioned for the show in New York. I picked up my sides—one scene was Steve drunk, another was Steve hard-edged, the third was Steve just an easygoing guy. I decided to make really strong choices, especially the drunk scene, because opportunities like this don't come along too often. I had to make this opportunity count.

"I did the drunk scene last. I played it very

broad, very inebriated. I felt it was the best I could do, and I left without thinking too much about it. I called up my agent and asked, 'Anything else going on?' A week or two later I was on the plane to California. I was going to network"—auditioning for the bigwigs at the Fox network—"knowing that if I got the part I'd stay and shoot the pilot, but if I didn't get the part it would be a looooong flight home.

"We arrived, these two other New York actors and I, and we all rehearsed with the director of the pilot"—Tim Hunter. "We were fine-tuning our readings for the parts we were up for. I was the third, and Tim was running out of time. Hurrying out, he said I didn't need much work: 'Don't worry, what you did before was fine. Just give it to me again.' That seemed like a backhanded compliment—I was doing a great job, but somehow he didn't have much time for me. Actors are really insecure people! I felt maybe I was falling by the wayside because he hadn't left any time for me.

"What eats me most is when things are out of my control. I didn't sleep well that night. I got there at eleven o'clock, went into the executive building, walked down the hallway. There were about fifteen people there waiting, and two of them were guys also interviewing for Steve. One of them was much bigger than me and blond. The other was smaller and dark. Obviously the producers didn't know exactly what they wanted for Steve Sanders. The other two guys went before me again. That's what has happened all my life, given that my name starts with Z. I'm at the end of the line, always. I'm used to it now, I guess.

"The first guy went in, and while the door was open this big shaft of light poured out, like it was some divine light. It seemed like the first guy took an eternity in there while the second guy and I waited. Number two was doing push-ups and karate kicks—anything to get a handle on his anxiety. I was trying to control myself and not let myself get anxious in any way. You keep thinking, 'You're at a level few reach. Don't let dry mouth or nerves get in your way. Breathe through it. I'll be damned if I'll let that happen to me!'

"When the door opened after number one was finished and the light radiated out of the room where everybody was, and they said, 'Ian, you're next!' all that control I'd been working on flew out the door. Out the doooooor! My throat went *boingggggg!* Dry mouth! Suddenly there was this huge lump on my tongue, like when you see the cop lights jump into your rearview mirror.

"There were like eighteen people in this small room. The heads of Fox, the heads of Spelling, and in the corner, the Man—Aaron. I was under the microscope. It was the longest pregnant pause I've ever . . . had the opportunity to create! I had a little system overload, but then I said, 'So? Are we ready?' That broke 'em up a little bit, got a chuckle out of them, and I knew I'd be able to deliver what I'd come to deliver. I got laughs from my drunk scene.

"I left the room, and number two was still out there. 'Ian, how'd it go?' he asked.

"'Great!' I said with a big smile. I looked him in the face. 'Great!'

"Take advantage of the psych-out factor. When you're an unemployed actor, you become cutthroat. You use all your tools. If he'd gotten as far as I had, I'm sure he was there for a reason, and he must have done well, too.

"I went back to the hotel and met up with the two other actors from New York. We ordered diet Cokes and pizza. Ten o'clock came around. The other two got 'we're sorry' calls, the 'thank you, but we're going in a different direction' calls. 'You're wonderful, but . . . ' calls. I didn't hear a thing. I was having a hard time holding it together, I can tell you. Hardly slept. Woke up with a stiff neck from tension.

"Then at ten the next morning my agent calls from New York and says, 'Ian . . . ' and from his tone of voice I knew it wasn't happening. Then he said I got the job and I literally flipped! I did a somersault on my bed! I was *so* excited! I haven't stopped smiling.

"I feel so lucky. Lucky that I got to be considered for the part. Not everybody who wants to be seen for a part is actually seen. I was lucky that I got the pilot. Lucky that the pilot was picked up. Lucky that the show is a hit. Such a one-in-a-million shot."

Ian's own take on the life-versus-art question is that "There are very few similarities between Steve and me. I guess we do look the same! We do have a common sense of humor. I find things funny that he does. He does things I might have thought about doing but didn't. I'm a helluva lot more responsible than he is—but the kid cracks me up!

"I actually feel more like Brandon than Steve.

The stories are similar. I'm from another state, a stranger here in California. My home town in New Jersey, West Orange, is more diverse than Beverly Hills. There are wealthy people and middle-income and blue-collar people. We all got along, whichever side of the tracks we came from. There's a more realistic view of life there, not just one slice."

Ian has always been a showman. He was just being himself one day in a grocery store when a talent manager felt the rays emanating from the little blond kid and encouraged his mother to put him on the stage. Ian was twelve.

He recalls this time in his life: "I started very young. When the three o'clock bell rang, I'd stick my head out the window, and if my mother's car wasn't in the parking lot, I knew I had the afternoon free. But most of the time it was there, and I knew I was shlepping in to New York for an audition or a modeling job.

"Because of my acting, I wasn't able to participate in sports. But in eleventh grade I decided I wanted to be on the swim team. I gave up some auditions to do it. I was the kind of athlete who was all-around but never excelled at anything, the second or third pick, that sort of player. I was good enough to be a swimmer. I did the fifty-yard freestyle and the two hundred meter individual medley. We won some meets.

"I had a hard time in school at first because I was diagnosed dyslexic in the first grade. I met with a special education teacher until sixth grade, to condition me out of seeing letters inversely. I benefited, and eventually I caught up to my reading level and higher. But it left its mark on me—even today I'm less likely to pick up a book than a tape. I like to get my information and entertainment visually and aurally, rather than from reading." Ironically, one of Ian's worst courses was public speaking. He got an egregious D. "My teacher and I just had a personality conflict," he explains.

"My friends in high school were Chuck, Larry, Bobby, and David. I knew them from Cabana Club Day Camp. It was a nice place, but not in the Beverly Hills Beach Club range. Those guys are still my best friends.

"I did some things in school maybe I shouldn't talk about. I went to Mountain High in West Orange. We were the Mountain Rams. Mountain's big rivals were Livingston High, the Livingston Lancers. There was this big rock on the border between their town and ours. The big thing was to paint your school's colors on the rock the night before the big game, so you'd have your colors on the rock during the game. Mountain's colors were black and gold. I think that big rock started off as a pebble and with thousands of coats of paint grew into that enormous boulder!

"One year I was hot—I did thirty-five commercials that year when I was fourteen. It got so that if I walked into an audition all the other kids would bum heavily. I was just booking everything that year. I was an outgoing kid with a very American look. I had straight hair and wide blue eyes. I was very appealing, I guess. My favorite commercial was for Fruit of the Loom. The guys who were the Fruits were all comedians—they laid me out! Fifteen hours with the Grape, the Lettuce—system overload!

"Fame is fleeting. One year you're hot, the next you're not, in the commercial world. That year was mine, my year in the spotlight. I did a hundred commercials all together. I learned concentration and perseverance. In commercials, you do things over and over and over. I saved enough to pay for college. One of the things I had in mind from the start was to buy my parents a new car. I told my Mom I'd get her a Mercedes when I was rich and famous, just to say thanks. It turned out to be a Chrysler LeBaron. She put ninety thousand miles on that old Buick to get me to my jobs and auditions. They didn't want me to buy them a car, but it was a big goal of mine and I insisted."

Later, Ian used some more of his earnings to buy himself a town house in Morristown, New Jersey. The mortgage was $2,000 a month, which he thought he could cover. But suddenly he stayed unemployed longer than he'd planned to. He went fifteen months without a job and was on the verge of bankruptcy. He crawled back to his father and got the loan he'd been too proud to ask for before. But he delayed cashing the check for a week. In that time he got a job and was able to give his Dad back the uncashed check. A close shave.

Ian didn't work just in commercials. He was also in daytime dramas like "Love of Life" and "The Doctors." He played Brooke Shields's younger brother in *Endless Love,* which costarred James Spader. Ian doesn't remember how young he was when he made the movie, but says he was "old enough" to appreciate the leading lady: "Being with Brooke for nine weeks would put a smile on any young man's face. That lit me up a little."

He also appeared in stage productions like *Peter Pan,* touring in Philadelphia and Boston. He spent six months on the Broadway stage, singing, and dancing in *I Remember Mama.* All through his childhood he took acting, singing and dancing lessons. He worked with tutors often and turned in his homework by mail when he was on the road. But, he recalls slyly, "Sometimes it was easy to get out of the work." He wound up with a 2.5 GPA in high school. "I took a beating there," he admits.

"There was never any question about college. I was going, and that was it. My father is an educator, working for the Newark Board of Education, and he made sure I had something to fall back on. My older brothers went to college, and it was a natural progression for me. I'm very glad I have my degree." Ian went to William Paterson College in Wayne, New Jersey, and earned a B.A. in dramatic arts.

"My second two years of college I worked on 'Guiding Light,' the soap, playing a character called Cameron Stewart. It was a struggle. I convinced my teachers to let me try to continue, even if I missed some classes. With their help, I was able to work full-time and still graduate on time with a 2.75 GPA. Not too bad. My parents were there with tears in their eyes when I graduated. My father went, 'Attaboy, Eye.'"

Ian's name is pronounced "Eye-un" instead of the usual way. It's got something to do with his mother's search for names starting with the letter *I* to honor her recently deceased father Irving. She knew about Ian, but the sound of it didn't do anything for her, and she thought it was stronger-sounding if it was pronounced "Eye-un." "I'm happy with my name," Ian says. "It's interesting, uncommon, raises a lot of questions, a good way to break the ice: Ian Andrew Ziering."

There never really is any ice when Eye is around. He's your friend from the first eye contact. He's close to all the men in the cast without seeming like some strange animal to the women. He says, "Being on the 'Beverly Hills, 90210' set with these guys, it's hard to think of it as a business. Everyone is so friendly, it's more like a family. We have this family feeling—which fades immediately when they call 'Action!' Not everyone is fortunate enough to do something they love.

"I hang out with Jay and Luke. I spend time with some of the girls once in a while, but I'm real tight with those guys. We go on personal appearances together and club-hop together. Just hang out and party, unwind after a rough day.

"The three of us just went to the Charlton Heston Celebrity Shoot, which is this major gun competition. I'm not a big gun enthusiast but Jay and Luke are and they turned me on to it. There was lots of bonding going on. It's a male thing. I shot shotguns and handguns and made it to the handgun finals and ate a lot of raw beef, being really manly. I'm just kidding! About the beef. I really did get to the finals, and I'd never shot a handgun before.

"I got the crap beaten out of me by that shotgun. I'd never fired a shotgun before. I came home and my eye was black-and-blue and my cheek was swollen and my left shoulder was a sight. Manly bruises. When I came to work on Monday, everybody thought I'd gotten into a fight. I said, 'Nah, nah!' Next time I won't make the same mistakes. Jay's team won the handgun finals, and his prize was a Smith & Wesson .45. There was a drawing and Luke won a .357 Magnum. I hit sixteen out of twenty-five pigeons, which they tell me was pretty good. What did I win? 'The winner is Ian Ziering,' and I go see what I won, and I won a trap, like for trapshooting, the thing that throws the clay pigeons. Jay and Luke were all jacked up. We're going to go out into the desert and do some trapshooting. We'll rig the trap to throw Heineken bottles instead of pigeons.

"Jay and Luke don't go anywhere without me. One time we flew up to San Francisco for Gabrielle's birthday. Gab had invited us but didn't expect us to show, but we did 'cause we love Gabrielle.

"If I go on an event with one of the girls, I feel very protective. I like to make sure they're not encroached on or grabbed at. Because of that, it's actually better if we don't go together. It's not so good for us to be acting like a big brother all the time, or for them to have to be big sisters to us, which they also tend to do."

In addition to hanging out with the other "Beverly Hills, 90210" cast members, Ian's unwinding activities include skiing and horseback riding. Perhaps being an ex-swimmer has something to do with the pleasure he gets from maintaining a massive saltwater fish tank in his town house. Then again, perhaps not.

Wait! There's more! "I've got this little motorcycle, a YSR-Fifty. It looks like a huge racing bike, but it's just fifty cc's, and it's no faster than a moped. I drove it over to the set one time, and Jay and Luke were driving it around the building. The girls had a scene in the hallway and we were waiting around for a long time for them to finish so we could do our scene. Jay grabbed the bike and said, 'Enough of this.' Jay rode it down the hallway of West Beverly High and stopped and yelled, 'You could ride a motorcycle through this scene!' and drove off.

"It's a young cast—how could you not have a good time? For one scene, we were going to a tuxedo shop. It was in the prom episode. First we did the master shot of all of us; then we did the close-ups. In my close-up, I'm watching Brandon trying his tux on, and I'm supposed to say, 'Not bad! Not bad!' So I'm standing there just in the right position for the lights, and I'm supposed to be looking at him. He's standing right beside the camera. I come to say my line, and he's standing there in his boxer shorts. After that scene, I'll tell you, I chased him around the building!

"I'm having too much fun here. So many side-splitting laughs with these guys. You shouldn't be allowed to have this much fun."

But there's a thoughtful side to Ian. His analysis of Steve is penetrating: "Steve is wealthy, spoiled. He can have anything he wants, materially. But he's an adopted child. His mother is a TV star. She doesn't have time to nurture him, so he has grown up without knowing right from wrong. He does know that he has lots of money, and he can use it to get out of sticky situations—or into them!

"He's a scammer. He's a prankster. All he's seen of life is glitz and glamour, so he's very shallow. 'Everyone cheats,' he says. 'Take advantage of it or be left behind.' He's on the edge of what is real and what is an illusion, which is somewhat typical of life in Beverly Hills. I don't know how well Steve would do outside of Beverly Hills without the facade of money to hide behind.

"Sometimes he shows his sensitive side. When it breaks through you realize he's not such a bad guy." But Steve knows there's something wrong with him. He calls Brandon a good guy at one point, and Brandon calls him a good guy back. Steve gives him a long, skeptical look.

In contrast to Steve, Ian had a happy childhood. His own parents have been married for forty years. Steve, on the other hand, "is overcompensating for a lousy childhood," Ian says. "His parents have been married and divorced twice—to each other—and he's grown up on his own. No one taught him responsibility. What he knows he knows from TV and seeing his mother in the business world.

"What he gets from his friends are the most important things in his life: compassion, companionship, understanding and support. His friends know what he's all about. They love him even though he can be a bonehead.

"As an actor you look for levels beyond the one dimension. Steve has those other levels."

By this time, Ian is back inside the studio, having shot a scene or two. He's been talking next to the craft services table, the spread of snack goodies that is always available on every TV or movie set. "It's our chozzerai," he says, using the show biz Yiddish word for "junk." "You just have to look at that table to gain a pound!"

Just then, Gabrielle walks by and can't help putting in her own two cents' worth: "Does he talk more than me? Ian talks a lot, doesn't he!"

"Get outta my interview, will ya?" Ian says.

Gabrielle adds: "We're both from New York," as if that explains it all.

"For instance," Ian says, resuming his analysis of Steve, "he hits on Andrea Zuckerman, but only because he's horny. It's a growing-up scene for Steve. I get some emotional stuff to play. We're going to see Steve coming to terms with who he is. There are some interesting episodes coming up. A lot of kids like Steve never learn—that's the unfortunate reality. I think Steve does learn—the hard way. He'll do something to set himself back, but he keeps coming back, forces his way back, and the others can't help but love him because he's such a character. I think our audience realizes that even though the characters have well-off backgrounds, there's a lot about them that's universal, and so they can relate to them.

"I have a story idea for Steve that I hope the show will buy. I've got it all written. It's about his reaction to some people in a nursing home. He gets in a jam and tries to buy his way out, and one of these old guys tells him that the only way out is through your family. But ironically, Steve doesn't have a family—not a real family."

The story idea comes from Ian's own experience. "I worked in a nursing home. I have a ninety-one-year-old grandmother, Bubby Fay, in a nursing home. She still has most of her marbles, and I speak to her all the time, and I see her whenever I go back east. Some of the others in that home, dumped there by their families, they're lonely and they've become embittered.

"I feel very disjointed out here in California. My roots are deep in New Jersey. I had been out here several times looking for jobs before 'Beverly Hills, 90210.' I couldn't get the time of day. Being on a hit series opens doors. People out here look at you and behave according to what you can do for them. It disgusts me, how so many people out here look at what you are, not who you are. I can't tolerate that. It's so phony! Be my friend because of who I am or don't be my friend at all! So you can imagine, it's been hard for me to find friends here. I guess my best friend outside of the people on the show is Carl Evans, who was with me on 'Guiding Light.' He's from New York, and look at where Luke and Jason are from— Ohio and Canada. Does that tell you something?

"I went to a nightclub once with Carl. There was this big line outside. He prompted me to 'go throw the weight around,' as he put it, with the doorman. I don't like 'throwing the weight around.' I don't really know how to 'throw the weight around.' This is all very new to me still. This line, though—it was about a year long! And it was a cold night.

"I went up to the doorman, this huge, imposing guy. I stood in his face for about five minutes. I finally got his attention and said, 'Hi, I'm Ian Ziering. I moved here about six months ago to play Steve Sanders on 'Beverly Hills, 90210.' Back when I was in Jersey, I was always wondering if there was any truth to the myth that when you're a working actor in Hollywood, you just cruise through a line like this? Is there any validity to that?' He looked at me and said, 'Yeah, c'mon in.'

"I was thankful to get in, but I have to be truthful: I can't deal with the elitist mentality. Yet I guess I'm a hypocrite, because I took advantage of it. Once you buy into it, once you start thinking it's what you are that matters, instead of who you are inside, then you're doing what my mother warned me against— letting the tail wag the dog. It's all downhill from there."

Ian's big laugh booms out. Not many guys would tell such stories on themselves. But he knows how easy it is to fall off the high wire. The betting is on Ian Ziering to stay in one piece. Whatever, he'll be laughing!

Gabrielle Carteris came in with it all. She has the perfect look for Andrea Zuckerman. She understands the character thoroughly. Gabrielle has the tremendous self-confidence that Andrea needs. Gabrielle really is a sixties liberal living in 1991, which is exactly what we wanted. She's good at playing Andrea's false front, which says you can't get through to her, while hinting at Andrea's reality, which is that she's dying for a relationship. Not much is said, but Gabrielle shows that Brandon is the guy Andrea is always hoping she'll date.

—AARON SPELLING

Gabrielle is so much like her character that some people can't believe Andrea wasn't written for her. Andrea is a very mature character. Gabrielle is more fun-loving and venturesome. She's as smart as Andrea, but she's got a much larger fun side.

—DARREN STAR

Being from northern California via New York, Gabrielle is prepared to play the outsider aspect of Andrea. She has the range to show the vulnerability of Andrea as well as her intensity. It's a subtle line to walk between Andrea's keeping her distance and her desire to be part of it all. Gabrielle can handle whatever we throw at her.

—CHUCK ROSIN

Gabrielle Carteris

GABRIELLE CARTERIS (RHYMES WITH "FAR Paris") is known as Gab on the nickname-happy "Beverly Hills, 90210" set. And Gab does have a tendency to talk. Her physical and verbal energy is irresistible. She's always in the center of the action on the set—chasing Jennie around the scenery, discussing life with Jason, gabbing with Ian.

Her character, Andrea Zuckerman, knows she doesn't fully belong in Beverly Hills or at West Beverly—she uses a fake address. But among the "Beverly Hills, 90210" cast of outsiders, Gabrielle, an outsider from northern California, is in with the rest of them. Andrea can be a moralizing nag, always bringing Brandon up short or forcing him to be more aware of the world outside West Beverly.

Gabrielle has a few hobbyhorses—she'll burn your ear off on the subject of education—but mostly she's all for live-and-let-live tolerance. And Andrea, in her wire-rimmed glasses, is emotionally somewhat repressed. Gabrielle, on the other hand, lets her feelings out almost before she has them.

Her account of how she won her part is a good example of her tendency to want to know all and tell all. She bustles into her PR company's office and immediately asks every question she can think of about this book. (Here's your answer, Gab!)

Eventually she gets steered back onto the subject of herself and blasts off: "I came from New York for the pilot season. I'd done that twice before without success. One time when I was in Los Angeles an agent told me, 'Gabrielle, this business is about tits and ass, which you have neither of. So it'll be very difficult for you in L.A.' But I decided to come out here again when a friend said she'd just got an apartment and I could stay with her free.

"'Beverly Hills, 90210' was the second pilot I auditioned for. I was going up for the part of Brenda and I got a callback to read for Tony Shepherd, who does casting for Aaron Spelling's shows. I was soooooo nervous! I was the first to audition. Mr. Shepherd came in and got very upset because the audition space was too small. But the actors finally went ahead and read for him. I read for both Brenda and Andrea. I was worried that Mr. Shepherd had been so upset about the space problem that he wouldn't even notice me, so I looked at him as I left and said, 'I hope your day gets better.' I think saying that to him made him, just for a moment, really be there with me."

That's typically Gabrielle—always upbeat, always stirring the pot. Then came the day to read for Aaron Spelling himself. Gabrielle describes her bird's-eye view of how a TV mogul runs his business: "There were about twenty or thirty actors all in this one big room downstairs. We were up for several of the parts that hadn't been cast yet. Lots of different types and races were up for Andrea, because the producers didn't know how they wanted to go with her. Oh, my God, it makes me so nervous just to remember it! Five of us were taken upstairs together, and then three of us went into this other room. Then two of us went into another room. Then I was taken out and ushered into Aaron's office."

Spelling's office is a thirty-by-thirty-foot space with picture windows wrapping around two walls. A long, long, long couch sits against one other wall. "There were all these people sitting in a row on the couch. I didn't know any of them, and I didn't know which one was Aaron. I did my first scene. I did so badly! Then I did another scene, which was better. Then I went out to change costumes and I quickly asked, 'Which one was Aaron Spelling? Which one was Aaron Spelling?' When I went back in, I was able to look at him.

"Then I got the call to go to network"—the stage of television casting where the producer's preferred candidates compete against one another for jobs in front of the network bigwigs. "By this stage you've signed the deal memo, committing yourself to the show if they decide that they want you. I went into this little room full of people in suits, women and men. Some of them didn't have room to sit down, and they squatted against the walls." It was Nervous City, because casting decisions not only affect an actor's life for the run of a show, which can be five years or more, but set the direction for his or her whole career.

"I was there to read for Brenda, so I brought along a picture of my brother Jimmy and me together because I'm a fraternal twin, like Brenda. I thought that might help them see me as Brenda more easily. I showed it to these people, and nobody laughed, nobody smiled. No one said anything. It was like a tomb.

"'Go ahead,' they told me. So I did my scenes, and I didn't feel bad because I did my best. I went home. I didn't get a call until a week later, after I'd caught a cold because I was so nervous, and I was feeling awful. The call was to come back again to read for Andrea. All this time I'd been studying Brenda, not Andrea. I stayed up until one-thirty memorizing Andrea's lines, forgetting them, and memorizing them again, agonizing and just going over and over the lines.

"I got to Fox and I was so nervous I had to get down and do sit-ups in the hallway. People looked at me and I said, 'Look, we all have our ways of warming up and this is mine, okay?' There was another girl there who was up for Andrea. I knew she had been working hard for that part for a month. I saw her and I started to cry. I wailed to my manager,

'This tension is too much!' Then we went over my lines again for the millionth time, and I instantly got control again.

"I went in to read. This was the second time I'd seen these people, so I said, 'Hi, everybody! Glad to see you again!' Nobody smiled, nobody said anything. They don't want to give you any false hopes, so they try not to respond to you. When I did my reading I changed one of the lines in the script and that made them chuckle. They called me back in and said for me to be 'even more sharp' the second time. After we'd all finished we sat outside the room where they were discussing us behind the closed door. Then they all came out. None of them would look at us.

"Later, at my manager's office, I was waiting with two other clients of my manager who were also up for parts in the show. They were hoping to be cast as Brenda and Brandon. The call came in that I'd gotten the part of Andrea. I got down on my knees and cried and cried, sobbed and sobbed, and laughed and laughed. Then I controlled myself, because the two others hadn't heard—they eventually were not chosen.

"I went back to New York and told my friends that I'd be leaving and I thought I wouldn't be back. I'd been offered a role in another show, but I really wanted to do 'Beverly Hills, 90210.' I'd only gotten the role for the pilot, but somehow I knew that even if the show didn't 'go to series' my life had been profoundly changed."

The show has now become the center of

Gabrielle's life, to the extent that she did nothing during the six-week break between the show's first and second seasons except publicize the series.

She explains her total involvement in "Beverly Hills, 90210": "The show has been really great for me. Before, I never felt really pretty. When I was younger I cut all my hair off. I looked like a little boy. People in the industry initially shied away from working with me because I looked so butch. 'Gabrielle, we really like you, but you're not pretty enough'— they said that to my face. One big agent in New York actually said, just when I was starting out, 'To be honest with you, Gabrielle, you're not very attractive. You'll never go far, and you'll always be second best, so I suggest you leave the business now.'

"At times I thought she was right. I'm not the typical beauty. But on 'Beverly Hills, 90210' I've found a strong sense of self, even though my character isn't one of the glamorous beauties. I feel really pretty now. I've got a real sense of confidence now about myself. I don't feel like this goddess or anything, but I like the part of me that's inside more than I ever have."

Like all of the characters on the show, school newspaper editor Andrea has grown significantly. When Gabrielle was called in to give an "even more sharp" reading for the character, she defined Andrea for the executives as "not bitchy, but matter-of-fact, cold-edged, all business-business-business," Gabrielle recalls. "But as time went on, the writers have rounded off those edges.

"By now Andrea has blossomed. She still gets

that edge; she still asserts her strong sense of right and wrong. She can be preachy, but she does it so honestly that you can't dislike her for it. She's got a real drive to learn. She's still a fighter, a survivor in a difficult situation. She wants to create her own life against all odds. She's struggling to be heard, so sometimes she's a little short on diplomacy.

"But now she's involved socially, she's exploring her sexuality, and she's not so much of a loner. She's learning to like herself, and she's learning that she doesn't have to be alone to be successful, so she's reaching out to people more.

"At the beginning Andrea had no friends. She met Brandon, and they immediately clicked. At first there was some hard feeling with Brenda. Andrea never took Brenda seriously, thinking she was just one of those girls who only like to wear nice clothes and never care about important things. Then, on the 'rap line' show, Brenda saves a girl who'd been date-raped, and I develop a new respect for her. Andrea also got to know Kelly and her problems, and I began to respect her. As much as others had points of view about Andrea, she had wrong points of view about them. After a while she stopped feeling excluded by the fact that the others have more money, and she realized the others were just people and became friends."

Gabrielle's favorite episode was last season's slumber party. "You really got to know the characters," she says. "A lot was revealed. The truth game broke down Andrea's wall when she couldn't lie about herself. It was a stepping stone to future story lines for her, especially when she had to be more honest about her feelings for Brandon."

Andrea has always had a passion for Brandon, secret at first, more open now. In the beginning she was a second conscience for him, provoking responses from him, like "Why do you have to edit me all the time?" And "You're just too good to be true, aren't you?" Now, though, Andrea doesn't have to hide behind her righteousness.

Gabrielle says, "Slowly, men are coming into Andrea's life. One time Steve and I were studying for the SATs, and he kissed me and told me I'm pretty. Then there's the thing with Brandon. There have been a lot of requests to see Brandon and me together. That might happen. It's great to have that 'Moonlighting' feel about Andrea and Brandon, the feeling that it's almost going to maybe happen. And if it starts to happen, then it should stop happening— and go back and forth. Also, this year I'm having the beginning of an affection with a young teacher.

"Andrea is letting people like her. She can see that people can like her for her intellect. She doesn't have to be blond and act ditzy. People can like her for who she is. She can hang out with the others without always judging them. She can be more fun."

Gabrielle's high school experience was very different from Andrea's. She was involved in issues, but she was also a leader in the lighter side of school life. As for similarities, Gabrielle remembers, "Like Andrea, I really loved school. I always spoke up for what I believed in, again like Andrea.

"The difference between Andrea and me is that I

partied and did a lot of things she wouldn't do. She's more resolute in what she wouldn't do. I was more willing to explore. Sometimes I got myself in trouble, sometimes I didn't. Now Andrea has grown to be more similar to me, and I can incorporate more of myself into her. In turn, she makes me more able to say what needs saying sometimes.

"Actors resist being identified with their characters. I've never felt just like any of the characters I've played. I wouldn't have to be insane to play a madwoman. I'd just use the part inside me that's crazy—and we all have a part like that. We are everybody in the world. People watch Andrea or any successful character on television and say, 'God, she's so real. I really understand her. I've felt that way myself.' And the reason is that they see parts of the character in themselves."

Gabrielle's school was Redwood High School in Marin County, north of San Francisco. Born in Phoenix, Arizona, she grew up in Greenbrae, California. "Redwood High was one of the best schools academically in northern California," she reports. "My background was similar to many of the others at Redwood. I was very popular there. I was a cheerleader and I partied and I got good grades. I studied hard and I played hard.

"Andrea appeals to a lot of viewers because there's a part of everybody that feels a little misunderstood. I connect with Andrea because at Redwood, I appeared to be very popular, but I always felt there was a part of me that people didn't know. I felt there was a part of me that was different from the norm, even though people thought I was completely normal. In that way I'm like Andrea. She's someone who doesn't feel like everybody else, and as she grows she's learning you don't have to be like everybody else to enjoy them.

"Let's see, what else did I do in school? I was a real participator. I danced. I was involved in gymnastics. I did a lot of volunteer work. I always had the attitude that I could create whatever I wanted in my life. I don't believe in thinking negatively. I believe you can have what you want in this world without compromising yourself.

"I came from a family that was divorced; a lot of others didn't. My family always really supported me. I went to school with my twin brother and always had him to share hard times and good times with. When we were little, we had a secret language only the two of us could understand. As we got older, we became very different people. Unlike Brenda and Brandon, we weren't very close in high school. I was always the scholastic one, and he was more of a rebel. Our SATs weren't identical! Now that we're older, we're still very protective of each other, and we tell each other things we wouldn't tell anyone else in the world. We're best friends."

As for Andrea, "She doesn't have a sibling—or I should say, we haven't met any brothers and sisters yet. We haven't fully actualized her family yet. I think we're going to meet her grandmother soon. Another difference between Andrea and me is that I got to study in Europe. Andrea has probably never left the San Fernando Valley other than to take the bus to West Beverly.

"At Redwood I never hung out with just one group. I had friends who partied a lot, friends who were into getting high—though I wasn't—friends who were very scholastic. I was like the hippie cheerleader. My hair was wavy, and I wore holey jeans, and to this day I don't know a thing about football. I liked cheerleading because we got to dance and perform, not so we could go out and toilet-paper people's houses.

"I liked to perform. I did ballet for eight years. I worked six to eight hours every day when I was young. I danced and went to school and didn't have any social life at all. I finally had to face the reality that I'm too short"—five feet one—"for a future in dance. So instead I did gymnastics and cheerleading!"

And Gabrielle worked. "We were financially all right—I did get that year in Europe—but not wealthy. My mom worked really hard to support us." Gabrielle's mother runs her own business—two clothing shops, one of them named "Jim-Elle" after her twins. Today, Jim is his mother's partner in the business.

"Jimmy and I shared a Toyota Corolla while some of our friends rolled around in Z's and 'Vettes. I hostessed in a restaurant. I had a job selling hot dogs for a while. I helped manage a Hickory Farms store, the youngest they ever had.

"Oh, yes! I translated for the deaf. I read a book about Helen Keller, and that first interested me in the problem. Then I had a deaf friend, and when I was in junior high I worked as a volunteer at a school for the deaf." She translated for deaf students when they attended classes with hearing students.

"Anything that's a challenge, I'll do it. I'm very ambitious. I love doing things that girls haven't done before or no one my age has ever done before. Life is a real opportunity, and I really think I can do anything. I'd climb a mountain if someone told me I couldn't."

When Gabrielle went to Europe in her sixteenth summer—not at fourteen, as some accounts of her life have stated—she learned mime and traveled with a mime troupe to Czechoslovakia, Germany, Austria, Switzerland, France, and Italy. When she came home that fall to California she taught mime skills to friends and performed "in coffee shops, on the streets, wherever, even on TV," she recalls.

"I was so upset one time about an issue that was on the ballot in my home town that I organized some skits and shows to help win the election. The issue was to allow the schools to fire a teacher if he was accused of being gay—that's so narrow-minded! Like, you can't have sex on your back! Or you're bad if you like brown-haired people. We raised a lot of money to defeat that proposition, and it was defeated. I felt good that I had contributed. I've always felt very strongly about persecution of people because they're different.

"I think back about that, and I can't believe I did it. I did it because I didn't know any better. I didn't know I couldn't do it. People often are hindered by fear and by knowing too much. If you know you simply can't do something, you won't even try to do it."

That was Gabrielle's junior year. Afterward, fearing that she would be typecast in her acting, she gave up mime, despite her success. "I didn't pursue it because you can get typed as being just a mime." To gain experience as an actor, she spent a year in the youth program of San Francisco's premier theater group, the American Conservatory Theater.

She had avoided high school drama. "The actors were a snobby group at Redwood, and I didn't want to be 'amongst the thespians.'" At Sarah Lawrence College in Bronxville, New York, just north of New York City, Gabrielle began acting at the beginning of her freshman year. "I did it badly," she admits. She did summer stock at Williamstown, Massachusetts, where Broadway actors go to work on their tans and up-and-comers go to carry spears and learn their trade. She spent her junior year of college in London studying at the Royal Academy of Dramatic Arts and the London Academy of Music and Drama. Nearly every successful British actor has trained either at RADA or at LAMDA.

And Gabrielle got her college degree, studying psychology and theater. "Every actor should go to college," she advises. "A lot of them get so wrapped up in their own success that they stop school. It's a real tragedy for some. Acting is such an immediate gratification business. In Los Angeles you can become a fad actor. You can be in one minute, 'out' the next. What if your career ends after a few years? You can't do anything else. You've given yourself no options. You should take the chance to grow as a human being. If you're a good actor, you'll have your success, whenever it happens. There's nothing worse than a stupid actor."

Gabrielle got into acting because of an older neighbor kid who wanted to be an actress. "We used to put paint cans in her backyard and put boards on top to make our own stage. We had spotlights, and our families came and we'd perform. Sometimes we wrote our own plays and lip-synched to records. Once I played Barbra Streisand, my brother played Al Jolson and our friend played Liza Minnelli. The performances were always instigated by this other girl, because of her ambition to be an actress.

"Somehow acting became something I pursued. I never felt it was the only thing I could do. I like the challenge of it, not the show-off part. Exposing yourself to the public can sometimes make you very uncomfortable. When I go on talk shows, which is part of the 'Beverly Hills, 90210' job, I don't tell anyone I know. The technique of being an actor is a continually fascinating challenge. What makes show business hard is the business side of the show. You have to get your performance past the business people's opinions before you're allowed to really perform."

Gabrielle's main credit before "Beverly Hills, 90210" was four months on the daytime drama "Another World," playing a runaway named Tracy. She has also appeared on after-school specials like "What If I'm Gay," "Seasonal Differences," and "Just between Friends." She has worked on the off-Broadway stage, notably in *Les Liaisons Dangereuses*. Her first film was *Jacknife,* starring Robert De Niro;

She played College Girl in Bar.

That was then. Really performing now, some of them for the first time in their lives, the young actors on "Beverly Hills, 90210" exude that glow of the Chosen Ones. They have that Members Only feeling. They're in the club, and you're not. No one glories in her membership more than Gabrielle.

Of her fellow club members, she says, "The guys on this show are the funniest guys I've ever been around. They're always playing and showing off. And the girls are great to be around. I can be serious—'It's time to work now, guys!'—and I can be playful. I love being with these people!

"Ian and I both came out from New York, so we had that in common. We're also both Jewish, and that was nice because I didn't have my family to celebrate the high holy days with.

"Luke has grown a lot in the last year, and he has so much stronger a sense of himself now. He's such a nice guy, very loving and nurturing. He has a pet pig named Jerry. He used to bring him to the set and we'd all hang out with Jerry the Pig.

"Jason was the cast member I did most of my work with last year. He was very supportive. He can take a joke, too! Jason has this particular way of clearing his throat before a scene. I used to mimic him and absolutely drive him crazy!"

Jennie Garth is perhaps the cast member Gabrielle spends the most downtime with. She recalls, "Jennie helped me find my apartment when I came out here. I didn't know my way around the city, and I took three days to look for a place. I woke up very early each day and drove around. I looked at twenty or thirty a day, all of them so boring. I was lonely and confused. I took myself to lunch the third day and I called Jennie and I was crying and she said, 'Come get me right now.' I picked her up and at her suggestion we drove right to the place where I live now"—zip code 91403. "We walked in and I said, 'I'll take it!' I feel I could always call on Jennie."

Gabrielle and some other "Beverly Hills, 90210" cast members had a high time last summer visiting England, where the series is even more popular than it is at home. "We arrived and we were all really jet-lagged, but I insisted that we go to the theater," she recalls. "So everybody else agreed to humor Gabrielle. We went to a play starring Peter O'Toole, but we all fell asleep sitting there! Two rows of us, all with our chins on our chests. One of the others looked back and saw that I was nodding off, too, and that was like a signal that we all could leave.

"We went to pubs and clubs. It was a wild group! I bumped into Jason and Ian in this pub, with women absolutely surrounding them! One was telling their fortunes. Those guys were peacocks with their feathers showing. Then we all went to a club and danced, particularly Shannen. She just went for it! Wild!"

Gabrielle, very much a "now" person, does little thinking about the future. She says, "I'd like to do films. Someday I'd like to have my own series. I'd like to direct. I'd like to write children's books. But right now we're so busy it's hard to think of anything else."

Yet even with her killing schedule on "Beverly Hills, 90210," Gabrielle spends time several days a week with a high-wire artist training for "Circus of the Stars." Shannen, Jennie, and Brian have also performed on this live TV special. Gabrielle says, "I've never been the kind of person to say 'I can't do that.' I like to do everything. I just go ahead. I like to face my fears—it makes me stronger. High wire? Just teach me, I'll do it."

The same with people. "I have friends all over," she says, "different types and different religions. I went with one to a Buddhist temple and chanted, with another to church and sang gospel. I'm very easy. I like a lot of things. If I see that something moves and touches people, I want to share and experience it, too. It's a joy to discover how other people live.

"Everything in life I've received is because I've taken a chance. Every time I give up comfort and security, good things happen."

David Silver just insists on moving in on the big guys at West Beverly. Give him a video camera and he'll shove it up everybody's nose. Brian Green personifies the underclassman he plays. But there's so much more to him—vitality, looks, dramatic ability. And this kid dances better than half the pros you see on MTV. We didn't have to teach Brian much. The more we gave him, the more we realized he could do.

—AARON SPELLING

Brian is one of those who's close to his character—in age, anyway. He's a delight to watch. At first we had very little for him to do. So we made him the school deejay. We gave him a video camera. Finally we gave him some drama to play, the episode with his grandparents in Palm Springs. He played it to the hilt!

—CHUCK ROSIN

Brian is the opposite of his character. He plays a nerd, and he's a stud! He's a very hip guy, and he's incredibly energetic. We saw him dancing last year at the cast Christmas party and he was so incredible we had to showcase him dancing on the show—he got to win the dance contest. There's a lot more to Brian, and we've just scratched the surface so far.

—DARREN STAR

Brian Austin Green

BRIAN AUSTIN GREEN IS A LOT MORE WISED-up than dweebish David Silver. He's older—all of eighteen!—and smoother, but he's still friendly and eager to please. Don't ask him for an autograph if you're majorly shy, because he insists on having a conversation while he writes his best wishes.

Go into the restaurant where he's scheduled a sit-down with you. Another TV personality might slam-bang in and announce loudly, "I'm Brian Green. Show me to my table!" Brian, wearing his T-shirt proclaiming "World Famous KROQ"—L.A's top New Wave station—sits on the step outside and waits.

Talking about himself presents no problems for Brian, who has a direct circuit from his brain to his mouth. His ideas and recollections spill out quickly. You need fast ears to follow him and a fast shutter speed to watch him, because he's not one to sit still and meditate.

Ready? Go! "I was on a slow streak after 'Knots Landing,' which I was on for four years plus. I got the chance to read for a part in 'Beverly Hills, 90210' and I felt right away that I could be David Silver—not just *do* David, but *be* David. This was one job where I could just be the character—it would be easy! They didn't know what they were looking for, but they knew it when they saw it! Sort of like me with girls. Anyway, Aaron Spelling was there to see me, and I got cast first of all the characters. That meant that when they were auditioning the Steves and the Scotts, I read with all the kids trying out.

"David and I have a lot in common. When I auditioned, I just went in and behaved the way I did myself when I was a freshman. David is a high-energy kid, and so am I. He just never lets people alone. He's always in a person's face, and I can be that way. We're different, too. He's a little geekier than I am—I should hope! David is insecure about himself. Out of the freshmen at West Beverly he's maybe the coolest, but he wants to be popular with the older kids." Brian says he never cared about his degree of coolth when he was in school. "If somebody likes me, they like me. I don't do things to make people think I'm cool.

"The thing about David, he doesn't know he's a fool. He imagines that people see him and see the way he dresses, and they think, 'God, he's cool!'

when they're actually thinking, 'What a geek!' He hasn't found himself yet. He doesn't know who David Silver is. He only knows what he wants to be in the eyes of other people.

"He has a hard time at home because of his parents' separation. It's hard for him when he has to go back and forth between them. That's made him uncomfortable with people, especially because he's going to a new school. Plus, he's younger than the other kids, so he has to be home earlier at night and he feels a little left out of the whole school scene sometimes. To compensate, he makes himself the deejay and the election mediator and tries to fill all the positions he can so people will notice him and think he's cooler than he is.

"The reason he wants to pal around with the older kids is that he's impatient. He's not going to get anywhere hanging out with the other freshmen. That's not going to do it for him. He's got higher visions than the rest of them. He wants to move to the top as fast as he can, to get the higher visibility he wants. I wouldn't be surprised if David wound up as president of the world someday! He has high, high ambitions. Every school has a kid like him.

"David will learn. He will get less uncool. Not too cool—don't worry! He won't lose the things that make him fun to watch.

"David does have a maturer side. It comes through every once in a while. There was the episode where David took his friends down to his grandparents' house in Palm Springs. He ended up fighting with the grandparents because he didn't want them around. But the rest of the kids liked them, and he had to face the fact that he was being a selfish jerk.

"David and Kelly are finally having some conversations talking about real stuff, instead of him just driving her crazy and her blowing him off. He learns about true friendship. When her mother and David's father have a date, she's horrified that I might become her stepbrother. The person she dreads most in life! And when I think about it, I'm horrified, too, that my true love is going to be my stepsister. So to torpedo this thing before it starts, Kelly becomes the stepchild from hell. In this scene in a restaurant, she tries to get her mother and David's father apart by being really bitchy. So David lets her have it. You see the stronger side of David: 'Do you think it's easy for me? I don't want to deal with this either!' Somehow this conversation starts a good friendship—in an awkward sort of way, because David is an awkward sort of guy.

"The other kids tolerate David because they have to. He's never going to go away, no matter what they say or do. Steve says to Jennie at one point, 'Just humor him.' And that's what they do, because it's easier to humor him than get rid of him. They don't want to be friends with him but they're stuck with him because they know he's never going to stop bugging them.

"I knew a kid like David in school. The funny thing is, he ended up being one of my best friends toward the end of high school. He would keep coming up to me saying things like 'I loved what you did on "Knots Landing" last night. I just loved it!' Or 'That commercial you did, wow!' I was going, 'Gee, thanks, can I get on with my life now, please?' This kid never stopped."

Brian's real-life situation was thus not too different from what happened to his character in the first episode of "Beverly Hills 90210." Remember David trying to glom on to Steve by complimenting him on his actress mother's latest performance?

"This kid I knew at school never stopped bugging me. One day I just said to him, 'Hey, you only want to talk to me because I've been on TV. You know, I'm not just an actor. We can talk about something else and have regular conversations.' So we talked a little more, and oddly enough we ended up friends."

Brian has no problem with friends now. There's always action in his dressing room, because if Brian isn't socializing with people in the cast of the show, he's hosting some buddies of his from the musical world. Brian sings, plays rap and rock, and may someday have a parallel career in music.

"Most of my friends are also actors," he says. "They understand the work, so they're the easiest to get along with. You don't have to explain things when you have to go out of town for a couple of days. If I want to run down the stairs singing 'Mammy' backwards, I can do it. My best friends are three guys I always go on trips with. We're inseparable!

"I usually don't drive because my Bronco II is such a gas guzzler. We go over to Catalina or skiing at Big Bear or Mammoth. I'm not bad at skiing. I can get down almost any hill. I'm better at basketball. Sure, I'm short, but I'm actually better underneath the basket. I can usually post up against taller guys because I'm a good jumper. I like to go to the Lakers games with my friend Nick Adler. His dad is Lou Adler, who always sits with Jack Nicholson."

As for girlfriends, Brian says, "I haven't found that perfect girl yet. I don't even know what I'm looking for. I am looking, though! It's hard to say what the perfect girl would be. I'll tell you when I find her. It's gotta hit off right away.

"Being on TV makes it harder to find girls who really like you for you. If you were going out with someone and you heard she was telling all her friends, 'I'm dating David from "Beverly Hills, 90210,"' that would be a bummer. I don't want to be liked for my career."

Brian spends a lot of his downtime with Luke and Jason. "We shoot baskets on the set or we go in my room and play Blades of Steel on my Nintendo. Jason's a huge hockey fan. We hang out. After work, we go eat sometimes. Luke and I do events together, like signing autographs at malls. We're always paired up because we're both high-energy. He'll stand on a chair and wave to people, and I'll run around.

"We're both into radio. We do radio station appearances together. We joke around about starting our own morning show. Once a week, maybe. We'll call it 'Coffee with Luke and Brian.' But our schedules are too heavy, so we probably never will.

"Jason and I are 'the Bones Posse.' That's what they call us, 'cause we're both so skinny. We both like dancing a lot. We take work seriously, but once the camera wraps, we really like to have fun. Luke and Jason came by a club some friends of mine run called Ballistics. It's on every Thursday night at the Whiskey. There was a bad mob scene inside. There's no age limit at this club until eleven o'clock, so there were a lot of really young girls, like fifteen or sixteen. They went crazy! We had to escape out the back door and run down an alley to get away.

"Another time me and Luke did an appearance at Disneyland. We stood up on Tomorrowland Terrace, a stage that comes up out of the ground, waving. There were six or seven thousand screaming girls going berserk. I got so pumped up on their energy. You've never felt anything till you've felt that!"

Brian's and Luke's intensity almost boiled over one time when they were playing a scene in which they were on opposite sides of a poker table. "Dylan is selling all his stuff so he can keep on playing, but David wins and wins. It was so intense! The eye contact was constant. There was a lot of tension around the table. Afterward we had to cool off and talk to each other for about ten minutes. I felt like I was actually taking his money. I guess it came out great on screen."

Brian's high-intensity personality was evident almost from birth. But the way he looks at it, he's always been normal, and his parents treated him normally. "It's not good to stop a kid from being hyperactive or high-energy," he says. "A kid needs to learn. Kids want to do everything, to get into everything. I say, let the kid do it. Let him learn from experience. My parents never stopped me from being hyperactive. They just let me go, and I eventually started to calm down. It's falling into place.

"My parents were great. They were always really supportive and helpful. They brought me up to know the difference between right and wrong, but they'd never stop me in advance from doing something. They let me learn on my own. They might tell me it's dangerous to step up on the top step of the ladder, but then if I climbed the ladder they wouldn't stop me. If I fell, I'd learn. Today, starting out as an actor, I have a better head on my shoulders because of the way my parents let me grow up. I'm not a dumb little kid.

"Sure, I used to break things. I threw a rock through a window once. I paid to fix it out of my allowance, which was twenty-five cents a week. I didn't get anything for a year. So I learned about throwing rocks.

"I never really worried about money because the things I wanted seemed to pop up, for my birthday or at Christmas. When I got things, I took care of them, because if they broke I knew I wouldn't get replacements. That would be it.

"I was never spoiled with money. The money I earned acting—none of it went to me. It all went into the bank. The result is . . . I just bought a house! Because I saved up all my money. That's pretty exciting. Not many kids at eighteen buy their own house."

Brian grew up with two older half siblings, his

mother's children by an earlier marriage. His older brother Keith is now thirty and works in a car parts store. His sister Lori, twenty-seven, is a hairstylist. "No one in my family was ever an actor. My mother is a housewife and my father is a musician, a drummer. He used to tour. He was on the road with Glen Campbell and the Captain & Tennille. Now he writes and produces music for TV shows like 'The Simpsons' and 'The Fall Guy.'

"Naturally, I grew up wanting to play the drums. I bugged my father about it: 'Can I learn? Can I learn?' He said no, I had to learn to play the piano first so I could learn to read music. So I took piano lessons for five years, and thank God I did. Oh, he let me screw around with his drums, but he never taught me anything because he knew that if he did I'd quit the piano. Now I'm working on getting a group together. Me and three other friends are getting ready to do some demo stuff."

Brian's show-business career started when he was eleven. He recalls, "In grade school I went to a performing arts school on the campus of the University of Southern California—go, Trojans! Graduate students in the USC film school would come around to our drama class and pick kids for their student films. I got picked to do four or five of them.

"I told my parents I wanted to be an actor. They thought it was a phase, like playing the guitar or becoming a pogo stick champion of the world. So they told me to wait six months. If I still wanted to try to be an actor, I could. They thought I'd forget about it, but I didn't.

"So I got an agent and did some commercials. My big break was doing a PBS movie, *The Canterville Ghost,* with Richard Kiley. I was nine or ten. I worked for eight days with these top people . . . but then afterward it was back to the audition road and more commercials.

"I auditioned for 'Knots Landing' because Donna Mills needed a new son. I got the role purely because I looked a lot like Donna. That's the only reason I got the role, I can tell you right now, because it had nothing to do with acting ability.

"I did that for four and a half years. The character, Brian Cunningham, was a Goody Two-shoes, a real boring kid—like I was then. I was just playing myself, like most little kid actors. Very few kids that age can really act. They just say the lines, and they say them like they didn't really mean them, you know? The hard part is going on to where you really have to act, not be just 'Oh, look at him, he's so cute!'

"The 'Knots' character didn't have anything to do. He'd go to the movies. He'd eat. He always seemed to be eating. He was just there so Donna could have a son. They used to have to scratch their heads to find something for him to do. They wrote him into all the dinner scenes. One thing was that he liked to eat everybody else's dessert. I liked to do that, too. I burn off the calories in a matter of seconds!

"The job ended when Donna's character got caught in some kind of scandal and she had to move to Japan. Guess who had to move with her?

"So I was unemployed and on the audition road again." Brian got parts in a number of series episodes, like "Highway to Heaven," "Baywatch," "The New Leave It to Beaver" and "Small Wonder." He was in the "Baby M" miniseries, and he could be glimpsed in the feature *Kickboxer II.* He particularly remembers *An American Summer,* which he puts down as "a beach movie with Joanna Kerns. I still wasn't comfortable with acting. I didn't prepare enough, either. I wasn't serious about it.

"Then I did a feature with C. Thomas Howell called *Kid.* That was a great experience because I played a real character, not just myself—in fact, totally opposite. I played this kid who listens to heavy metal, wears long hair and a leather jacket— the whole deal. I was in Arizona for four months doing it, and I loved it. My character was Howell's sidekick in his quest for revenge against the people who murdered his parents. Well, the movie went straight to video, but I had fun, whatever!

"Then I was on the audition road again. I was finally serious about what I was doing. *Kid* finally pushed me over, to make me actually work on my profession. That's when I got 'Beverly Hills, 90210.'"

All this time Brian was attending North Hollywood High School— which is actually not very close to Hollywood. "North Hollywood was a regular high school," he says, "nothing special, no glitz. Your basic high school. No rich kids. Mostly middle class. Some blue collar. Beverly Hills High School has the basketball court and the floor opens up and there's the pool underneath. We didn't even have a school pool. The cool kids were the football players and the cheerleaders—what else is new? I never hung out with them. I didn't care about being popular. I had my own friends. By the end I just cared about getting the work finished and being done with it. I didn't really go to school.

"I spent a lot of time in studio school. That's where kids study directly with teachers on the set of the show they're working on. Studio school is hard. People think that just because it's only three hours a day it's easy. But that's three hours of work. At a regular school you do a lot of sitting around and hanging out. You're not necessarily participating. Three solid hours of one-on-one is tough. I was serious about school—I had to be because school was more important to my parents than my acting. And more important to me, too."

When he did attend regular classes, Brian recalls, "I was a lot like David at first. I was really insecure in the ninth grade. I would do anything, almost, to have friends.

"But I changed after I got to be friends with Corky Nemec. I met him at a Teen Beat trip to Palm Springs. We really hit it off. We listened to the same music and liked the same girls. We hung out together for almost a solid year almost every day, although now it's hard to see each other because of our schedules—he's just a little bit busy on his own show—'Parker Lewis Can't Lose.'"

"Corky is a real friend because he showed that

he really liked me for myself. I'll never forget one time we were going to the mall and I came out dressed almost exactly like him. I'd bought clothes just like his.

"He goes, 'What are you doing?'

"I go, 'Nothing.'

"'What are you wearing? Go put on something you like, something you'd wear.'

"When you've been going so long trying to impress people and here you have someone who doesn't care about impressions, it stuns you. He's a great friend.

"After that, I realized I was cool enough just being myself. I didn't have to be a different person. I went in to school for eleventh and twelfth grade with a different attitude: if you like me, fine, if you don't, fine; I'm going to be myself. I ended up with more friends than before because I was more sure of myself."

Now that Brian is eighteen, he's joining several of his elders in the "Beverly Hills, 90210" cast and becoming a property owner. He says it isn't to declare independence from his family—it's just that a man's gotta do what a man's gotta do.

"I'm not moving into my own house to get away from home and my parents. My house isn't far away from theirs. It's just something I've always wanted. I feel I have to do it. I have to see what it's like to be on my own. Also, they have plans of their own, and with me around it might be hard to take those vacations or move or whatever. I won't have a roommate. I might have my sister move in. She's trying to save up to buy herself a town house, and if she lived in my place she could save faster.

"Excuse me, what time is it? I better run. I gotta go close escrow on my house!"

Seeing Tori's growth as an actress has been one of the high spots of the year for me. She's turning out to be a natural comedienne. In the Spring Dance show, Donna wore this impossible hoop dress. She couldn't sit down in it! It wasn't a big bit in the script, but when Darren was filming the scene, he just held the camera on Tori for about two minutes. We were able to use all of that footage—throughout the dance we kept cutting back to Tori, because she was so funny. At the same time, in the episode where we discover that Donna has a learning disability, Tori handled the drama with aplomb and dignity. I'm impressed.

—CHUCK ROSIN

Tori went to Fox's casting director using the name of Tori Mitchell. She won a part that wasn't much of a part. Donna is the least defined of our principals. But Tori has defined Donna. She created a marvelous embarrassment for Donna, this seemingly perfect girl, who considers herself uninteresting to the rest of the girls at school. The way Tori plays her, she uses humor as a weapon. My proudest moment was her work in the Spring Dance show. Turning her little bit into a running gag—that was hysterical!

—AARON SPELLING

Being from Beverly Hills, having gone to school on the West Side of Los Angeles, Tori had all the right prerequisites for Donna, as the character was initially. She was a sidekick who had just a few lines. If she hadn't proven herself, that's where she would have stayed. She's made the part her own.

—DARREN STAR

Tori
Spelling

TORI SPELLING'S PERSONALITY DOESN'T LEAP out at you. A little at a time, it trickles out from behind her shy exterior. Then before you know it, you're both smiling and laughing and discussing something goofy like the latest gruesome horror movie!

Among the "Beverly Hills, 90210" cast, Tori is the quiet one. She dresses to not stand out. She understates herself in her manner and choice of clothes, confident that you'll see what's inside if you keep looking.

Tori is one of those Hollywood kids you never heard about when she was growing up. You never heard about her wild parties, her loud prima donna behavior, her difficulties with booze and boys. She just didn't have these problems.

She had a carefully protected upbringing as the daughter of the most successful producer in television, Aaron Spelling, and his wife Candy. Virtually everyone in Hollywood has worked with Aaron and the word on Tori all over town is "Nice girl. Reserved. Good head on her shoulders. Unspoiled. Surprises you. Still waters run deep."

"I find Tori very funny," says Darren Star. Darren is the man to impress if you want to have good lines written for you on "Beverly Hills 90210"— he created the show and supervises the scripts week by week.

Darren goes on: "Off camera, Tori is shy and very sweet. On camera, something else happens and she becomes a comedienne. She's carved out her own niche on the show, and we've watched her blossom on camera. You know, Tori had just one line in the pilot, and if she hadn't proved herself, that's all her character would have remained—Kelly's sidekick. Tori showed us what she can do, and we've exploited those abilities."

How unpushy is Tori? "Before the second season started," she says, "the producers talked with all of us. They asked us what we liked about our characters and what we wanted to see them do. I didn't have much to say. I just said, 'Write Donna some good story lines.'"

Tori has a PR rep, and that office is the place she chooses to introduce herself and talk about her life. She's wearing an ultra-washed-out denim jacket and pants. You have to really stare to notice the tiny diamond in the center of the gold chain around her neck. There's a street note in the dark blue baseball cap she wears. It's an Oakland Athletics cap, but she admits she's wearing it for the color, not because she's a fan.

What does she like about playing Donna Martin? "Donna is really funny," she answers in her soft voice. "She gets some good laugh lines. She's ditzy . . . snobbish . . . she's in the popular clique with Kelly, so she snubs the freshmen like Scott and David. She's money-conscious and into the social scene without really understanding what it's all about.

"Donna says what she thinks—but she just doesn't think very much! When Brenda thought she was pregnant, Donna didn't quite get it when Brenda said what her test results were, and she said, 'Oh, maybe you'll have twins!' She says things like 'My parents absolutely refused to get me a nose job, so they're buying me a new car instead!'

"Donna isn't intentionally mean. Kelly is more intentionally a snob, to be popular. Donna just follows her lead and doesn't realize how hurtful she can be. If she did realize it she wouldn't act that way, because she's more sensitive. She'd be sorry if she knew she was hurting people."

During the show's first year, as the show's producers noticed Tori's abilities, they started giving her interesting story lines. One involved Donna's learning disability. Tori recalls, "The way she found out about the learning disability was when she took the SATs and scored way low, like 600-something for verbal and math combined. Her friends did much better and she started thinking she couldn't hang out with them because they're smart and she's not. But it turns out that she's not dumb. Her problem is that when she sees something written and has a time limit for dealing with it, she gets nervous and freezes up.

"I totally sympathized with Donna because I didn't score very high on the SATs myself. I don't have a learning disability; I just didn't score very high. I did well in school, though. After I graduated last spring I decided to take a year off before going to college. I got into the University of Southern California, which is where I wanted to go. They'll save a place for me. The reason is that I need a breather from school, and besides, I couldn't go to college and be on the show, both. I'm definitely going to go to college."

Another episode showing a different side of Donna was the one this season in which she and Steve decide to play the stock market. "Steve wants Donna as a partner because she's real good with figures. I guess that ability comes from adding up her bills when she goes shopping!"

How does Tori sum Donna up? "Donna is very different from me. I'm down-to-earth and not ditzy at all—at least I don't think so! But she has become my alter ego. I arrive at the set, and I just slip into her like I was changing clothes. I don't have any model for Donna. I just use bits and pieces of people I've run into. None of my friends are snobbish or so much into the Beverly Hills scene as she is. A few of my friends are maybe a little ditzy, though—I won't say which ones!

"Beverly Hills ditzes aren't any different from ditzes anywhere else—they just shop more! Shopping—we gotta do it! It's my favorite pastime. I just go and look, and if I find something I like, I buy it. If I don't like anything, I don't have to buy something."

Tori's upbringing seems made-to-order for a part in "Beverly Hills, 90210." But she has a surprising viewpoint when asked if growing up in Beverly Hills gave her a head start on the show. "The others in the cast come from different backgrounds," she says. "They do sometimes ask me about specifics . . . proms and stuff like that. A lot of their questions I can't answer because my life was totally different from the scene at West Beverly."

True, not many people get nicknamed by Barbara Stanwyck. At first you might think that "Tori" is some kind of misspelling, but it's actually short for Victoria. Tori says, "My parents wanted to name me Victoria, but they thought everyone would call me Vicky and they weren't too sure about that. My Dad was real good friends with Barbara Stanwyck and she said, 'Why don't you call her Tori?' It was a good idea! Ever since then I've been called Tori."

Growing up around the stars and bigwigs of Hollywood never affected Tori because she never felt especially privileged. She says, "The way I grew up seemed normal to me. I enjoyed my school, which was Westlake School for Girls. It's where I wanted to go, and my parents wanted to send me—no problem. All the kids there were close, and none of them were snobbish. We had a group of about fifteen of us who were friends, and out of them there were maybe four I'd go everyplace with because we'd grown up together.

"Westlake was a place where you didn't have to wear makeup—just wake up, shower, go to school. We wore uniforms, so there was no clothes competition. There were no boys, so there was no boy competition, because there were no boys to fight over. Girls can be pretty ruthless when it comes to fighting over guys."

That naturally calls to mind the "guy question," and Tori's answer is: "What I look for in a boy is a sense of humor, mainly. Because I'm not a serious person. Humor, intelligence, looks—can't forget looks, can we? Someone who's honest. Someone who'll be there for me. Of course, my boyfriend fits all those categories. He's my ideal . . . as of the moment! Just kidding! No, we're real committed.

"Before, I used to like a guy who was a challenge. The ones who were into me, as soon as they liked me, I didn't like them. With this boy, it's different—not that he wasn't a challenge! It was mutual with him. It was the first time that happened. As soon as he started liking me, I liked him more. It was probably the first time that happened."

Tori recalls her school proms: "The junior prom wasn't so great, but the senior prom was nice. I went with my boyfriend, so asking a guy wasn't too hard. We went with five other friends and their dates. We took limousines to the prom, and afterward we had a big party. It was a lot more fun than the prom on the show. I had a red dress—not a huge hoop dress like on TV.

"I didn't miss anything in high school. I don't even want to hear about anything I might have missed going to an all-girls school, because I enjoyed it so much. We had a brother school, the Harvard School, which is an all-boys school. We had dances with them. Most of my guy friends were from there—though not anymore. It's funny—now all my friends are from the Valley."

The Valley is the San Fernando Valley, just on the other side of the Hollywood Hills from Beverly Hills. It's an overpopulated land of sunshine, smog, and wall-to-wall malls. Most folks from Beverly Hills never admit to going there. They'd rather be gagged with a spooooon, because the Valley is grody to the maaaax! Or so the area's reputation has it. But Tori is grown up enough to realize that there is intelligent life in the Valley.

Tori has friends on the show, too. "I'm probably closest to Shannen. We go out a lot—mostly shopping. Shannen is real honest. She's one person I can count on to tell me what she really thinks. She's great to go to for advice. If I have a problem with my boyfriend, she always understands, because she's wise beyond her years and always knows exactly what to do.

"Brian Green and I are the closest in age, so we hang out together sometimes. We're all real close, everyone in the cast. You'd think it might be difficult spending half your waking hours with these gorgeous guys, but they're actually pretty easy to be around. They may be beautiful guys, but to us they're just friends and co-workers.

"I was worried about working with so many young actors. I've never worked on a show where everybody was so young and so near to each other in age. It turns out that they're all great, like my second family. They're all there for you when you need them."

Like most of the cast and most actors in general, Tori grew up knowing she wanted to act. Being Hollywood born and bred, she had a chance to act on her impulse early. "Acting is what I always wanted to do," she confirms. "My dad took me onto the sets of his shows when I was a baby, and I grew up around the camera. One day when I was about six we were on the set of 'Vega$' and I told him, 'I wish I could be in this.' So he said, 'Do you want to try it?' He gave me one line in the show. I loved it, like instantly. The line was, 'Uncle Dan, do you want to come ice skating with us?' I said it right the first time and they didn't need a second take. They called me 'One Take Tori.'

"The next thing was, I told my Dad I wanted acting lessons. I'd had art lessons and other kinds of after-school stuff, but I'd never wanted to stick to them. I stuck to my acting lessons for five years. I had a private coach, Kathryn Daley. She came to our house a couple of times a week. She taught me how to feel more comfortable in the job. I learned things like how to pick up a script and do a cold reading. How to behave when I met casting directors, what they're looking for, how to give it to them. Just generally learning to battle insecurity, which every actor feels.

"As I grew up, I had a few guest appearances on my dad's shows. Pretty soon I decided I wanted to prove to him that I could do it on my own without depending on him, so I got myself an agent. Dad was real proud when I did get other jobs. I never did commercials because I already had a start. The first job I got on my own was an episode of 'The Wizard.' I was the girlfriend of the boy who was guest starring. I was ten or eleven."

Tori has also appeared in episodes of "Hotel," "Monsters," "The Love Boat," "T. J. Hooker" and "Fantasy Island." She has a couple of TV movie credits: *Shooting Stars,* with Parker Stevenson, and *The Three Kings,* starring Lou Diamond Phillips.

As for feature films, she says, "I did *Troop Beverly Hills,* with Shelley Long. I was one of the leaders of the bad girls' team, the Culver City Red Feathers. We lost the big event, and there was a big scene with lots of extras where I was supposed to bust in and steal the trophy and run off. We started shooting the scene and I ran in and grabbed the trophy, but I knocked the whole table down. I thought I'd spoiled everything, but the director was yelling, 'Great! Print! Perfect!'"

She describes her route to "Beverly Hills, 90210": "I learned about the show because my dad brought home the script. I read it and loved it and called my agent and asked her to get me an audition for the part of Kelly. When I went in to read for the pilot in front of the producer and director, Chuck

Rosin and Tim Hunter, I used the name Tori Mitchell. That was my dad's idea, so they wouldn't connect me with him. Well, like many others, I didn't get the part of Kelly. But they did offer me the part of Donna, and I took it. It was real small at first, but they've let me expand the part a lot."

Now, in addition to "Beverly Hills, 90210," Tori says proudly, "I've got a recurring role on 'Saved by the Bell' on NBC Saturday mornings. It's a cute half-hour sitcom about kids in school. I play a nerd named Violet Bickerstaff—see, I'm not typecast at all! I do all different things! In that show, I wear braids and glasses and I'm smart. I do 'Saved by the Bell' whenever I have time off from 'Beverly Hills, 90210.'"

But Tori has a secret passion only slightly connected to acting: writing. She says, "I like to write in my spare time—scripts and stuff. I never try to do 'Beverly Hills, 90210' scripts—I don't think I could write for the show. I'm too close to the characters. I wrote a screenplay last summer, 'Footprints in the Sand,' and I actually filmed it! It's being edited now and I hope to sell it to a cable channel like HBO.

"It's forty-five minutes, and I'm in it, too! I did it all—even directed! It's about four girls who grew up together and how they go in different directions right after high school. I patterned the main character after Jennifer in 'Days of Our Lives.' That's my favorite daytime show. In fact, I even named the character Jennifer! She's a strong-willed character who always speaks her mind. In my script she writes for a newspaper part-time while she goes to school and stays in the town where she grew up. She and her friends stay at this beach house during their last summer together.

"I got the production together myself. I talked to the casting director on one of my dad's shows to find out how you get actors. I learned how to approach actors' agents, and I got a lot of actors to come in and read for parts. It was great to be on the other side for once! To judge instead of being judged. It was real fun to look at a lot of them and pick and choose and say, 'I want that one!' Right now the film is being edited. The rough cut wasn't exactly what I expected, and now it's being re-cut.

"Dad looked at the script for me and helped me with the rewrite. He showed me how to simplify it. But he's not involved with selling it. I want to do that on my own. If it's not good enough to be on the air, I don't want it on."

Aaron Spelling says of his daughter, "She's so unlike Donna, it's amazing. I'm really proud of her, because she's a professional. I've had the greatest thrills a father could have because of her. We all went to the premiere of the film *Soapdish,* and there were lots of photographers at the door, and people were lined up across the street. They were yelling 'Tor-eeee! Tor-eeee!' The photographers said to me, 'Mr. Spelling, do you mind if we get some shots of Tori by herself?' And Tori said, 'Sorry, Dad.' I said, 'Tori, I love it!' She was so sensitive, to say 'Sorry' to me!"

Being her father's daughter is mostly a plus for Tori, but there's a slight downside. It's clear this is one tight family: "Dad has always been there for me.

He's real supportive. He and my mom were never stage parents. My career is what I want. Dad helps me when I'm getting ready to interview for parts. He never tells me how to do it. He gives me ideas for different ways to play scenes. You know what? He's usually right!"

Other people's attitudes, though, are sometimes difficult to deal with, she reports: "When I was little, there were kids who wanted to be my friend because of my father's wealth. You can figure that one out. One or two times I can remember kids coming up to me and saying things like 'Oh, my dad says your dad has this big house. Can I come over and play?' I was always skeptical. I mean, like, really! My friends now, they could care less.

"I always feel I've got to prove myself, particularly when I was younger. I wondered if people were thinking, 'Oh, she must be a little spoiled brat.' I was always shy. I used to sit quiet as a mouse and always do what I was told. That would be the first day of a job. The second day I'd see people's whole attitude change.

"A couple of times when I interviewed for jobs and did really well, I wouldn't get called back for a second interview. Or I met someone who was totally rude to me for no reason. I would ask Dad, and he'd say that person used to work on one of his shows and things didn't work out for him or her. So it's tough sometimes, but that's the way it goes."

Yet Tori's attitude has always been very positive. She credits her mother, Candy Spelling. "Yes, I do have another parent! Mom gets overlooked sometimes. She's great! I can talk to her about anything.

"When I was little, I used to make her come with me when I worked. She would sit there for hours. The other kids would have these pushy stage mothers, but my mother just sat there by herself. I felt bad for her, looking at her there sometimes, but she was happy to do it for me. I used to wake her up early in the mornings when I worked. I was so scared to death I'd be late to the set. If I had to be at the studio at seven A.M., I'd make Mom get me there at six."

So maybe there's a little overcompensating here? "Exactly. I'm real shy, and I don't express my feelings very much. Acting has helped me get over that. When I'm on a set or auditioning, I'm totally open and outgoing. Acting lets me be someone else. So if I'm somebody else, it's okay to be loud."

Tori's future is unlimited, but she tries to keep a close rein on her ambitions—at least the ambitions she wants to talk about. "My ambitions?" she says. "Stay acting. Write. Star in a horror film. Yes, that's my dream! I've seen, like, every horror film ever made. My favorite is *The Shining*. I like all the *Nightmare on Elm Street* movies. All those mindless ones, the more horrible the better. My mom loves them, too. Ever since I was little we'd stay up late together and watch horror movies. My dream is to be in *Friday the 13th* and be the one who survives and finally kills Jason."

"So far the Walsh way of raising kids has worked pretty well"

THEY'RE FORTY, GIVE OR TAKE A COUPLE OF semesters. His hands have gingerly touched the spreading baldness above his forehead. She has surely seen a gray hair or two. Their favorite music went out of style before their children were born. They have heard the chimes at midnight. They are . . . the parents!

If Cindy and Jim Walsh are traditional parents, then dinosaurs are traditional animals. Even in Minneapolis they must have stood out as old-fashioned. In Beverly Hills, they're museum-quality. They have given their sixteen-year-old twins every advantage, but two stand out: their means are moderate, and their values are firm.

The Walshes are unable to keep up with the

Joneses, Beverly Hills style. They can't buy Brenda and Brandon BMWs and Corvettes. Shopping is something they do when they need something; it's not a way of life.

These parents believe in two-on-two parenting. Mom and Dad should be aware of Sis and Bro's problems and be on the spot when help is needed. They should present the parental viewpoint, even when the two parents differ. Discipline should be imposed. Forgiveness should be dispensed.

Except for the Walshes, not much is seen of so-called normal households on "Beverly Hills, 90210." One reason is that the old definition of "normal" has changed. For instance, most American kids today are not growing up with their two birth parents.

Carol Potter, who plays Cindy Walsh, notes, "All the parents we know about on the show are divorced or separated. We don't know about Donna's and Andrea's yet. That trauma is now the norm. The Walshes are the exception. But I think the picture the Walshes present is a good one. There's a reason why it takes two people to make a baby."

Both Carol Potter and James Eckhouse, who plays Jim Walsh, are parents themselves, though their children are younger than Brenda and Brandon. Carol and James are unabashed fans of the show's intentions. "From all I've heard," Carol says, "parents think the show is terrific for their kids to watch. I can't tell you how many mothers have come up to me and told me how happy they are that their kids are watching 'Beverly Hills, 90210.'

"I have a friend of a friend whose daughter is so

crazy about the show that she taped and saved every episode. The mother had never seen it. Somehow she caught one episode and liked it. Then she and her daughter spent the whole next weekend watching all the tapes.

"The good thing about the show is that it opens topics for discussion. It touches on the things that are important. It's not so much that the kids watching are saying, 'I did this.' They're seeing the show as a what-if situation. It helps teenagers and parents break down that traditional wall of silence."

James Eckhouse says, "'Beverly Hills, 90210' is different—it's not as paper-thin as others. There's an element of reality to it, a sense that people have complicated problems that aren't easily solved. There isn't always an upbeat, rosy ending.

"Kids growing up realize that there isn't an absolute answer to every question. In real life things aren't always sewed up nicely.

"One reason the show became a success," James theorizes, "is that it had such low visibility at the beginning, in terms of media attention. We worked in the back closet because we were 'just another teen show' and we weren't 'destined for success.' Now that we are a success, there's more pressure on us. It's harder to keep that complexity."

The two older actors have similar opinions about the problems of holding to traditional values in a place like Beverly Hills. James says, "Beverly Hills has a glossy exterior, and the show invites people into that myth. But the show isn't really about that. It's more universal. Underneath, the show is about connecting; it's about communication.

"It's great that you've got this glossy, affluent surface full of beautifully clad people driving wonderful cars and playing with wonderful toys. That's not the way life really is. This show deals with people on the human level."

Carol says, "The Walshes set limits for Brandon and Brenda. Brenda was always asking for this or that, and her mother had to tell her that they couldn't keep up with the life-style of her friends' families. I think that the wealthier you are, the more important it is that your children learn the connection between money and effort. People who have too many choices too early tend to have problems later."

The constant battleground in the show is the Walshes' struggle to provide guidance without breaking off communication with their kids. Carol analyzes it this way: "The show's format is to provide information about an issue or a problem that teenagers face and then show one of the characters making a decision based on the information. It may not be the decision everyone would make, but it's the right decision for that character. Another kid might decide differently.

"I think kids need to learn to make decisions for themselves. If they're told every move they should make, they wind up unable to think for themselves later. I remember reading a study of girls who had been abducted by men in cars. The girls who obeyed these strange men and went into their cars had grown up under parents who had insisted that they obey adults without question. The girls who resisted and escaped being abducted were the ones whose parents had urged them to think for themselves.

Mr. Walsh is drawn in more traditional terms. "My character is from a fairly strict background. Jim Walsh was raised with strong values and a sense of the Christian work ethic. He values what's right and fair. Now, though, he's in a faster-paced situation with looser morals. He pulls back, realizing what he and his family are all about. The Walshes are from the Midwest; they have a strong sense of family values.

"Sometimes Jim Walsh can be a little overbearing. He finds himself being like his own dad. I find the same thing in my own life as the father of two kids. Sometimes Jim says things that are a little outdated. But he's learning. He's learning that his kids are human beings, not objects. The Walshes' children teach them about communication.

"What's great about the show is the sense of intimacy between the characters. Relationships go below the surface. That effect is achieved not just with the words in the script. It also comes from chemistry between the actors.

"I love the episode this season where Brandon gets the job with the high-powered guy he meets at the beach club. Jim is scared because he thinks he's losing his son. He sees Brandon losing his connection to the values he has tried to teach him. Jim gets more and more rigid. Finally, he sees that Brandon needs to make decisions on his own.

"Another favorite episode was the one where Brandon works to get a car. Then I really nail him about not taking the time to make sure the car is okay. I come down hard on him. Then I realize he's not a horrible kid. He's a wonderful person who makes mistakes like anyone. He's worked hard and deserves a second chance."

Like James, Carol connects her character with her own mother. "I model my character on my own mother," she says. "My mother was very clear on limits and boundaries. I'm a mother myself, of a four-year-old boy, so the parenting issues are very different from those Mrs. Walsh faces. My son Christopher is all over me all the time, but when kids get to be teenagers, they start developing a sense of self, and a lot of doors start closing. It becomes hard to know what's going on in their minds. The key is communicating. The best rule is to set and enforce limits, but never punish a child for telling the truth."

One problem with that rule, though, is that parents can't always tell when their kids are telling the truth. For instance, in the drunk-driving episode of "Beverly Hills, 90210," Brandon and Brenda both lied to their parents, or at least bent the truth. Carol says, "That's right, parents can't always tell when kids are telling the truth. Sometimes you just have to trust them. Mrs. Walsh knows that there comes a time when you've got to say that you can't do anything more."

Mr. and Mrs. Walsh often differ in their parenting approaches. They're usually shown in bed later, coming to terms. As Carol sees it, "Cindy Walsh is the peacemaker. She doesn't have much conflict with others. There's some realism there, because she's like my mother. My mother told me that I was a pretty good kid when I was a teenager, except for about two weeks in eighth grade. Mr. and Mrs. Walsh may disagree, but they talk. Mr. Walsh tends to lay down the law a little more than she does, which is not uncommon."

James Eckhouse agrees: "Cindy is a lot more communicative than Jim. She's more willing to be understanding, I'm more apt to jump into being strict. It's a real stereotypical situation, but then a lot of families are just like that. Jim has had more conflicts with both children than Cindy has. I sometimes still see them both as children. But usually during the course of an episode, I learn to communicate. Jim is confronting this age's demand that men be more sensitive."

Both "parents" enjoy working with the young cast of "Beverly Hills, 90210." James says sweepingly, "I wouldn't mind if any of the young people in the cast were my son or daughter. They're all so alive and creative."

Most of Carol's parenting scenes involve Shannen Doherty, and she says, "Building a relationship with Shannen was a long and gradual process. She's an independent young woman. She knows very much what she's about. She's close to her own family.

"I've gotten very close to her, closer than I knew! We worked late last night, and Shannen was nervous about finishing because she was flying off for the weekend on the red-eye to Chicago. She made her plane okay. I went home and had a dream about her. In the dream, we were driving together. She was going to borrow my Land Rover—but I don't have a Land Rover! A very funny dream.

"Jason is a bit older than Shannen," Carol continues. "He's a more back-slapping, fun-loving guy. He's fun to hang out with. Mostly, though, the kids tend to hang out together on the set. I call them kids, though most of them are quite a bit older than their characters.

"I have to work hard during our scenes to remember that their characters are just sixteen, because Shannen and Jason are such mature professionals. On the other hand, Shannen and Jason don't need someone to watch over them the way Brenda and Brandon do. They know when to lighten up.

"Sometimes I lighten them up without intending to. I'm constantly calling them by their real names during scenes. There was a big scene when we were backstage at the fashion show and Kelly's mom was freaking out on stage. My line is, 'Kelly, is she all right?' But I actually said, 'Jennie, is she all right?'

"Jennie burst out laughing. I had no idea why she had laughed during this big dramatic scene. I had to be told what I'd done that was so funny, and that made it even funnier. They tell me it was one of the funniest moments on the set last season.

"Another time, in a scene with James, I say, 'Whatever possessed us to name our twins Brandon and Brenda?' Except that I actually said 'Brendan and Brando!'"

James also commented on his youthful co-workers: "Jason and Shannen work in different ways. Both are very professional, though both can be headstrong at times because they know what they want—but not in a bad way. Both of them know who they are and have their feet on the ground. That's a good thing, because the pressures on them are becoming enormous. I feel very protective of them. Instant fame is what everyone wants. Now that they've got it, it's a tough road for them. I see them both stopping, taking a breath, and taking stock of themselves.

"I really enjoy my time working with them. It's a loose, playful set. Everyone is really professional, and at the same time we all want to have fun, too.

"Jason and I try to crack each other up. We'll do things like throw food at each other. Yesterday we were working real late into the evening and everyone was trying to stay on top of it. I was doing a scene with Jason in the Walshes' kitchen. I picked up this zucchini and stuck it down the front of my pants to crack him up. So he did the same thing. We were challenging each other to do the whole scene with zucchinis in our pants. We got halfway through before cracking up. You do some pretty silly things.

"Everyone on the set adores Jason. He's real level-headed, able to make everyone feel comfortable and at home. Although we goof around a lot, we've found a real intimacy and we have a wonderful time.

"Shannen and I don't joke quite as much as Jason and I do, because our relationship on camera is more serious—the daughter and the overprotective father. Still, we do have a great time on the set. She's always joking with me, making faces from behind the camera or pretending to be Daddy's nymphet."

Both Carol and James look forward to several more years of profitable parenting on "Beverly Hills, 90210." "I like the idea of working a couple of days a week, on the average," Carol says. "I can have a life and a career, too." James Eckhouse has his eye on the show's future: "Maybe Jim will get fired and have to work independently. Then it would be great if one of my kids came to work for me. Eventually they'll have to go off to college. I have a feeling that next year might be their last high school year."

Carol hopes the show will keep its sophisticated approach to issues. "Some people worry that the show puts ideas in kids' heads. My feeling is that unless you talk about issues, you're more likely to have eruptions of inappropriate behavior. I got a letter from a father who accused us of saying it was okay for his daughter to sleep with her boyfriend. But he hadn't really watched. We presented the issue as being a lot more complicated than that, and we said that for a lot of girls it's better to wait. The show always presents a long line of consequences of the characters' choices."

James goes further: "I think the show could hit kids' problems even harder. It's already a tough, complex society today. I'd like to see a stronger racial mix, certainly. I like the longer-running story lines we're getting this year, spreading issues onto four or five programs instead of squeezing them into one. I think the show can only get richer."

Back to school

WEST BEVERLY HIGH SCHOOL DOESN'T ACTU-
ally exist. But there's a beautifully designed old
school only twenty miles away that looks just the
way West Beverly would look if it were real. It's
Torrance High, home of the Torrance Tartars
(maybe a lot of dentists' kids go there!).

"Beverly Hills, 90210" shoots all its West
Beverly exteriors at Torrance. Before the cameras
roll, however, prop men carefully tack up the West
Beverly sign on the front of the building. And they
make sure no Go, Tartars! signs are visible.

Early this morning, the 150 people in the
"Beverly Hills, 90210" unit are encamped in the
school parking lot shooting scenes for the second
season's back-to-school episode. Behind the camera

seventy teenagers lounge around on the asphalt, awaiting the crowd scenes in which they will do their walk-bys, skate-bys, drive-bys, and bike-bys.

There's something very special about this parking lot asphalt, which is lying there so flat and unobtrusive. See that deep blackness! Note the smooth texture! Observe the straightness of the parking space lines . . . and tingle! Once, a few years ago, the crew that laid this asphalt and painted these lines included someone we all know today: Luke Perry. It was Luke's pre-Hollywood era, when he was just trying to catch a buck doing any job he could.

Today, though, Luke's blacktop days are long behind him. He's standing coolly about ten feet in front of the "Beverly Hills, 90210" camera, looking his natural best as a TV star! For this scene he's carrying a notebook and a doughnut bag, and he comes up to the motorcycle parking area. Dylan is a friendly guy, and he's spotted a new girl, name of Emily, who looks a little out of place. Guitars, black leather jackets, and two-tone black-on-blond hairdos like Emily's are rarely seen at West Beverly High.

Christine Elise, the actress playing the biker girl who's just moved to Beverly Hills from free 'n' easy Marin County in northern California, runs her getting-to-know-you lines with Luke. Dylan suggests ditching together, Emily declines—he was only kidding, anyway.

After Luke and Christine play the scene together for the camera, Christine plays it alone for her close-up. When close-ups are shot, actors who are in the scene but not in the shot stand behind the camera and deliver their lines. That's called "lines-off." Some actors recite their lines-off like zombies, knowing that their performance isn't being recorded. Other actors, like Luke, help their costars by giving something extra to their lines-off.

Luke being Luke, though, he does it Luke's way, not anybody else's way. While Christine is making the appropriate howdy-stranger expressions for the camera, Luke is behind the camera giving her geeky grins and weird words. He knows Christine needs all the help she can get in this scene, which is her entrance onto the show, and he's helping her energize her performance.

In the background of Luke and Christine's scene we can see Kelly's red 325i BMW convertible with beige interior and wire spoke wheels. Alongside it is Steve's Corvette convertible, jet black with jet black interior. The next scene to be shot actually comes earlier in the show—Kelly and Donna slink out of the Bimmer and greet Steve exiting the 'Vette.

Now is the hour for the extras to shine. The assistant directors corral the mass of kids they call "atmosphere." They distribute the bodies around the background of the scene by asking first for all the people born in March and April, then the people born in June and July, and so on. The extras are commanded to pretend to talk among themselves, but not actually to utter a word. We only want to hear the words of the stars in the foreground.

Two extras are playing catch with a Nerf football. There's a trio of hacky-sack kickers. A kid on a skateboard takes a noisy pratfall on the sidewalk, and the applause is led by the irrepressible Ian Ziering, standing up in the cockpit—I mean, the driver's seat—of the 'Vette. One of the Nerf football extras tries to throw the ball behind his back, and it thumps onto the hood of the 'Vette. The ball is confiscated. This is almost like real school!

At last the scene is lined up and the camera can record Kelly's scrumptious outfit, a red blazer over designer jeans and cowboy boots. Donna, overdressed as usual, is wearing an achingly ochre skirt and a stone-washed denim jacket. Inevitably, the dialogue of this scene involves clothes. "Nice shirt," Donna says, and Steve replies, "This old thing?"

Next to arrive for another junior year at West Beverly are the Walsh twins—you remember them? Brandon is behind the wheel of a classic cream-colored Mustang with wire wheels. Brenda is wearing a thirties-style tie and slacks with two-tone wingtips. Brandon wears his usual unpretentious jeans and collar shirt. The scene has dialogue in which Brandon and Brenda recall their arrival at this place exactly a year before.

The big time-consumer here is making sure Jason Priestley slots the 'Stang in just the right part of the parking place so that everything will be in focus. While the director and crew fidget and fuss, Jason and Shannen Doherty laugh and joke in the front seat of the car. "Questioning my driving skills, Attias?" Jason calls out to the director, Daniel Attias. He's responding to the director's worried look, a response to Jason's starting to back the car out for another take while Shannen's makeup artist was still applying that all-important last touch of blusher.

Afterward, all the cars are in place, all the people are in place, and the gang marches inside to start school. To shoot this walk-up scene, the director has chosen a Steadicam shot. This involves strapping a specially balanced camera onto an operator, who backs up in front of the advancing actors. The idea is to convey a certain amount of jerky immediacy without turning viewers cross-eyed. Steadicam shots are complicated and usually must be repeated a number of times before they're right. "Why am I in this scene?" Jason laments. "I don't have any lines."

Ian walks around singing the theme from "Rawhide." Luke, not in the scene, stands by, his shirt off, displaying his recent work in the gym. The actors walk back and forth, doing and redoing the scene. Jason calls out hopefully, "That's it! Put a button on it! We're outta here!"

The director asks the sound man, who has been bedeviled all morning by the noise of planes at nearby Torrance Airport, "How was it for you?"

"I'm speechless. It was indescribable!"

"All right! That's lunch! Thirty minutes!"

And so it goes.

Go back to the beginning...
See the 90 minutes that started it all!

THE BEVERLY HILLS, 90210 HOME VIDEO
available in video stores everywhere January 1992.